Complicated Souls

Berni Hellier

Disclaimer

This novella's story and characters are a work of fiction. Any resemblance to real people, living or dead, or events is purely coincidental. Counsellor training sessions are described but these are not based on actual events.

The opinions expressed about mental illness and childhood trauma are those of the characters and not those of the author.

ISBN: 978-1-5272-6543-1

Dedication

This book is dedicated to my amazing husband Jon who believed in me and encouraged me to keep writing even though I wanted to give up many times and to my two grown up children, Georgia and Luke, who have endured me talking about this book for way too long.
Lots of love, from me x

CONTENTS

"Monsters live within us,
sometimes they escape……"

Berni Hellier

ACKNOWLEDGMENTS

Thank you to my friends who encouraged me to write this book and to Dana for reading the proof and giving me the confidence to publish it. Thanks to Jessica Runyard who helped to edit the book and to Georgia and Dana for the final revisions.

KIRA 2010

Kira Devlin walked down the long corridor. The confident clip clopping of her heels concealed how she really felt, and her stomach lurched with every step she took. She walked past the group of teenage boys who loitered outside the engineering room. She ignored the wolf whistles that followed her. As she walked, she scanned the doors for room numbers. She reached room nineteen and paused with her clammy hand nervously gripping the door handle. She was not entirely sure that she was ready for this. She took a deep breath in and opened the door.

She scanned the large room. Her eyes were drawn upwards to the wonky chandelier that hung in the centre of the ornate ceiling. The walls were plastered with old leaflets and advertisements. In the far corner stood a large thirsty rubber plant which had obviously seen many groups of counselling students pass through. The room was full of mismatched armchairs set out in a horseshoe shape. Two larger leather armchairs were placed at the front, facing the horseshoe. At the back of the room there were tall built in bookcases heaving with dusty old books. The room looked tired and jaded and a musty smell hung in the air.

Kira sat quite close to the door, maybe subconsciously planning a quick getaway if this was not what she was expecting. A dark- haired woman whose smile took over her face came and sat next to Kira.

The woman introduced herself excitedly, 'Hi, I'm Leanne.' Leanne talked nonstop but Kira did not mind as it gave her a chance to get her bearings. Leanne talked about her three children and her husband and how she had tried for ages to get on the counselling course. Kira half listened to Leanne whilst simultaneously listening to some of the other conversations that evolved in the room; listening to more than one conversation was one of her many skills.

Keeping one eye on Leanne, Kira noticed a rather dishevelled middle-aged man come into the room. Kira heard him say that his name was David. He seemed eccentric. He wore old fashioned brown cords and the fronts of his shoes were scuffed and dusty and his wiry grey hair seemed to have a life of its own. Kira could hear him telling the others that he was a poet. Kira thought that he was self-obsessed and annoying from the outset. Next an elderly lady entered the room. She looked around seventy-five. She introduced herself as Megan. Kira liked her immediately. Megan was quietly spoken and calm, but Kira could tell that she was a confident and strong character. Megan moved slowly but Kira sensed that her mind was razor sharp. Megan had retired from nursing over twenty years ago but wanted a new challenge in her life Kira looked forward to getting to know Megan.

Gradually the room filled up with people. Introductions and small talk replaced the awkward silences. Kira made a mental note of each new person that entered the room, there were twenty students in total ranging in age from about twenty-five to seventy-five. The women outnumbered the men by four to one. There were teachers, nurses, social workers, a fireman, a stay-at-home mum, a poet and even a nun. They really were a diverse mix of people.

At exactly nine thirty, an internal door at the front of the room swung open and out stepped a rather wise looking older woman and a handsome man in his early forties. The pair smiled, made eye contact, and took their seats at the head of the horseshoe.

'Hello everyone and welcome to West Trinity University. My name is Nancy, and I will be your course tutor for the next three years. I would like to congratulate you all on getting onto the counselling diploma course,' she smiled.

Kira liked the look of Nancy. She looked as if she was in her late sixties and when she smiled her whole face crinkled up. Kira thought she seemed solid and trustworthy. Nancy talked for a while about the course in general and Kira felt herself begin to relax.

Then it was Michael's turn, 'Hello everyone and welcome. My name is Michael and I'll be your personal development tutor for the next three years.'

Michael was tall and athletic looking. He had green kind eyes that twinkled warmly as he spoke, he was also much quieter than Nancy. He had a strong calm presence that Kira liked. 'My role will be to support you and to help you to develop your personal awareness. Each week you will have personal development sessions to develop your self -awareness.'

Kira had no idea what personal development was, but she knew that the next three years would be an adventure.

TOBY 1985

Toby ran excitedly along the gravel path eager to get to school. School was Toby's favourite place, the only place where he felt truly safe. He liked the routine but more than anything he liked the way that his teacher made him feel. Miss Hartman always spoke kindly to him and smiled whenever she saw him. Today was particularly special though because today was Saint David's Day and Toby was going to get a prize for his dragon picture. He had worked so hard on his painting and was excited for the school assembly where he would be presented with his prize. His mind whirred with anticipation wondering what it might be. He had never won anything before, and he could not wait to stand in front of the other children. He was excited as he would get to sit on the special chair on the stage.

BANG! Toby tripped over a jagged rock on the uneven path and hit the ground hard. His palms skidded across the gravel and dust clouds floated up into the air. For a moment, time seemed to stand still. Just for an instant, there was no pain, just shock. Then, suddenly the agony struck and the pain in Toby's hands was searing. Toby looked down at the dirty broken skin on his palms. Bright crimson blood began to ooze through the dirt on his palms and Toby started to scream. He scrunched up his tiny face and gritted his teeth as huge tears bounced down his face plopping into the puddles in front of him. The pain engulfed him.

An arm yanked at his coat from behind.

'You stupid worthless piece of shit! Look what you've done to your trousers! I paid a fiver for them! I told you not to run you stupid idiot!' The arm gripped him tightly. The nails dug into his hand and he felt his feet leave the ground for a second. His mother was enraged. 'Stop that crying right now you big baby or I'll give you something to fucking cry about!' She poked him hard in the chest with each word that she spat.

Toby, although only five, knew that his only option was to control himself. His sparrow like chest convulsed as he struggled to stop the sobs, he bit hard on his bottom lip and avoided his mother's stony gaze. He had learnt that looking at her made her react worse. The rest of the journey to school was walked in total silence. Toby pretended he was a robot who could feel no pain; he imagined that his hands were metal shovels and that the dripping blood was just wet paint. The only way he could cope with his life was to use his imagination.

By the time they got to school the bleeding had stopped and the raging stinging in his hands had been replaced by a different pain, an emotional pain that Toby was able to feel but not yet understand. Toby entered the school playground where some of the older children were playing football, using their sweatshirts as makeshift goal posts. The younger children were playing tag, running in and out of each other. A red headed boy ran up to Toby and excitedly asked him to play, but Toby did not even answer. He was still shaken up from his fall. He just stood on the spot wrapped up in his own little world.

At precisely quarter to nine, Mr Harris, the headteacher came out and rang the bell.

Mr Harris had been teaching for far too long.

He spent hours on end daydreaming about retirement! Each day he counted down the days left on a calendar hung proudly in his office. He no longer enjoyed his job, and he no longer liked children let alone teaching them.

Hearing the bell, the children all ran to their lines, excited for the day ahead. Toby pulled his hoody over his head and trudged face down into his line. He stood at the back where he always stood. It was almost like he was not there. The other parents all waited to wave their children into class or blow kisses. Toby's mother was the first to leave. She did not even enter the school yard, she just left Toby at the gates so she could finish her fag (smoking was banned in the school grounds). She did not even look back to see Toby go into school.

BOUNDARIES 2010

At precisely 9:30 am, the office door at the front of room nineteen opened and like clockwork out stepped the tutors. Nancy swished into the room flinging her grey checked shawl extravagantly over her shoulder.

'Today's teaching session will focus on boundaries,' said Nancy. 'I want you to work in groups to decide what boundaries you think are important in the counselling situation.' Nancy organised the students into groups. Kira was put in a group with David (the poet), Leanne (the talker) and Megan (the wise one). Ann (a retired violin teacher) joined the group too. Each week they did different collaborative activities and each week they were allocated different roles, and today it was Kira's turn to be scribe and spokesperson for her group. Nancy handed out flip chart paper and marker pens to each group. Kira knelt on the carpet and wrote the word 'Boundaries' on the top of the flip chart. Without speaking she scrawled the words 'physical' and 'relationship' on the chart.

'Time,' said David... 'I think that you have to make sure each session runs to time otherwise it may get too intense for the client.'

Kira scribbled 'time' on the list.

'Space?' suggested Ann.

'What about emotional boundaries?' asked Megan.

Kira began to mull the suggestion over but before she could complete her thinking David spoke,

'Huh!' he said throwing his head back in disagreement as he did so. 'How on earth can you counsel someone if you keep an emotional distance! Don't even bother putting that one on the list!'

Kira was irritated with his contemptuous manner. He was such a know it all and always so condescending. Before the group could argue it out Nancy was clearing her throat to get everyone's attention,

'OK everyone, it's time to share your ideas with the larger group now please.'

Within minutes everyone had got up off the floor and back into their seats and everyone settled down to see what the other groups had come up with.

Each smaller group took turns to feed back their ideas to the larger group. When it was Kira's turn, she confidently rattled off the items on her flip chart. She got to the word 'emotional' and hesitated. She knew she would have to say this diplomatically but did not want everyone in the main group thinking that she agreed with David's idea.

'Well we were undecided, Megan suggested emotional boundaries, but David disagreed,' said Kira. 'He believes that counsellors should not have any emotional boundaries.'

David sat there looking smug.

Nancy glanced up over the top of her glasses which were always halfway down her nose and Kira thought she saw a glimmer of surprise on Nancy's face.

'OK,' she said, really drawing out the k sound, 'what do other people think?' she asked looking eagerly around the room. Kira knew exactly what she was doing; Nancy was looking to the group to challenge David's extreme ideas.

David however did not seem to get what Nancy was doing. He spoke first.

'Well I think that counsellors should not have any emotional boundaries. How can you really feel what someone else is going through if you barricade yourself up emotionally?' He sat there confidently not expecting anyone to disagree with him. Silence flooded the room.

Then Matt decided to speak. Matt (the fireman) was a quietly spoken serious looking man.

'I disagree with David… I think that we have a duty as counsellors to ensure we protect ourselves emotionally. We are going to be working with a lot of troubled people and we can't afford to allow their emotional chaos to become our own.'

Matt's comments opened the flood gates and within minutes everyone was arguing about the extent to which counsellors should have emotional boundaries. Nancy smiled to herself as she listened to the debate. She looked at her students with a sense of pride.

Eventually David turned to the tutors and asked what they thought. Nancy turned to Michael,

'What's your opinion?' she asked.

'Well,' mused Michael curling his index finger across his top lip, 'I believe that you have to be careful. Some clients may have attachment issues and they may have issues with boundaries. I have worked with many clients who have borderline personality disorder - a disorder often caused by experiencing trauma or abuse as a child. One client tried to destroy me, to cut my self-identity into tiny strips until I no longer knew who I was as a person. He wanted complete control of me - it was emotional terrorism. My supervisor saw what was happening. I was blinded by this client's extreme emotions and charisma. So, I would say, you must imagine an invisible shield around you to filter what gets to you; you need some emotional distance to protect yourself and the client.' The colour drained slightly from Michael's face as he recalled this difficult memory, and his eyes turned to the floor.

Nancy looked around the room, she immediately picked up on the atmosphere in the room. She could see that some of her students were shocked by what Michael had just shared. Nancy cleared her throat and addressed the group

'What you have to remember though is that clients like this are exceedingly rare. You are highly unlikely to come across anyone who is so extreme. Michael was unfortunate. Having said that, you must remember that you will be developing very intimate relationships with your clients and some clients could develop unhealthy attachments to you… so Michael's right, you need to keep your wits about you, you need to be mindful of the relationship and keep yourselves safe.’

DESERT ISLAND 1986

Toby sat bolt upright in his bed. His eyes widened with fear. His bedsheets were soaked through and so were his pyjamas. He sobbed quietly to himself, he knew that at six years of age he should not still be wetting the bed, but he could not help it. The panic inside him began to rise. It surged from his feet to his head in a wave making him hot and flustered. He rifled desperately through his cupboard drawers to find the hair dryer. Hands shaking, he switched the hair dryer on. He frantically waved the hair dryer over the sheets and the stained mattress, willing them to dry. He knew that he would be in big trouble if she found out that he had wet the bed again.

Suddenly, his bedroom door swung open. A shadowy silhouette filled the doorway, her heavy shoulders and top-heavy figure filled the door frame. Toby braced himself. She was enraged. He could sense it. He prepared himself for the onslaught. Her hands were clenched on her hips and Toby could almost feel her anger. She lunged across the room and grabbed a clump of hair from the back of his head.

'You dirty little bastard! I'll teach you to piss the bed… you do this on purpose! You dirty little bastard!'

'No Mam! Please Mam! Please don't hurt me!'

She pulled his head backwards and then plunged his face deep into the soaking mattress and held him there. Toby screamed inside his head - he thought he was dying, but he had learnt that panicking or retaliating just made her worse. She was pushing his face down so hard he could hardly breathe, as the stench of ammonia filled his flared nostrils. Toby remained still and limp for ages praying for the torture to end; he felt as if he was suffocating. Then she yanked the sheets from the bed and tore Toby's pyjamas off him, throwing them in a heap on his bedroom floor. Toby silently gulped in some much-needed air as she turned and left the room, leaving him naked and trembling in the dark.

Toby sobbed silently stifling his pain. He felt desperately sad. He closed his eyes and went to a different place, a place that he often visited in his head. He imagined that he was on a desert island, safe and alone; where he lived in a tree house and could hear the waves lapping on the shore, where he had mischievous monkeys for friends. He imagined eating fresh fish and climbing trees to get coconuts. He pretended that he had a loving mother who cherished him and never hurt him. Miss Hartman's face flashed into his mind and he felt better. Eventually, after a few hours of living in his imagination, he fell to sleep, curled in the foetal position, shivering on the cold damp sheets.

STALKERS 2011

Kira was looking forward to the day ahead. College days were always so interesting, they somehow felt like time out from her real life. However, they were by no means easy days. They never failed to stir her emotionally, and there would often be fireworks between her colleagues, and heated arguments would ensue. Sometimes the teaching matter would trigger some of her peers and things often got heavy. She walked the familiar corridor towards room nineteen. She entered the room and quickly scanned her surroundings to see who she could sit by. She glanced at the whiteboard. The title of the PowerPoint caught her attention - 'The effects of childhood trauma'. The digital clock flipped to 9:30 and like clockwork, Nancy and Michael entered the room. Nancy warmly welcomed everyone, and they began the old familiar check in routine. Each week the students would 'check in'. Some students talked about their lives, some students shared how they were feeling, and some students talked about what was on the news. Kira liked the regular check in session, although she sometimes struggled with what to say. She listened attentively as her peers told funny stories, shared painful emotions and mundane happenings from the previous week. Leanne talked animatedly about her new puppy and how he had eaten her sports socks and chewed the leg of her new dining table. Megan talked about social deprivation and political issues. David talked about the counselling course and the poems he had written that week and Kira felt herself glaze over.

Eventually it was time for the teaching session. Nancy introduced the subject gently,

'Now before we begin, I want to warn you that some of you may find this topic difficult, indeed, some of you may have suffered from childhood abuse yourselves. If anyone needs to leave the room at any point, please feel free to do so. Just get up and leave, go and get some fresh air or grab yourself a coffee.' Nancy began by talking about the impact of neglect or abuse on a young child, 'Sometimes children dissociate as a means of coping with the trauma that they are going through or have been through.'

Kira found the idea of dissociation intriguing.

'Dissociation is a state in which one becomes removed from reality. It can take the form of daydreaming, running on autopilot or general disconnection from actions. Basically, it is the child's way of protecting themselves from the horrors of their lives. Adults have the choice of flight, fight, or freeze. Children do not usually have the option of fleeing from their abusers because they rely on them for their basic care needs. So, instead, they retreat into their own little world. You will often see traumatised children staring into space, apparently daydreaming. Some children take this coping strategy with them into adulthood. In extreme cases, they can develop multiple personality disorder or borderline personality disorder. Severe childhood abuse is sometimes called 'Soul Murder' because of the devastating detrimental damage it can cause.'

Megan, the older lady cleared her throat,

'Nancy, I'm slightly going off on a tangent here, but is it correct that people with Borderline

Personality Disorder are more likely to become stalkers? I once had a friend who was stalked... and the fella that stalked her had Borderline Personality Disorder.'

Nancy then entered Borderline Personality Disorder into Google and displayed the results on the whiteboard so that everybody could see them.

Borderline Personality Disorder is characterized by persistent difficulties with interpersonal relationships. Many individuals with Borderline Personality Disorder have difficulty forming appropriate attachments. They may fluctuate between idealisation (intense admiration) and devaluation (anger or hatred).

'This obviously has implications for stalking,' said Nancy. Looking around the room at the shocked faces, Nancy looked concerned, 'I don't want you to see people as disordered and problematic, although I have to concede that some individuals are so severely affected that it leads to problematic behaviour or even mental disorder.'

Kira felt uneasy. There was a sense of fear or dread rising inside her that she pushed back down, all this talk about abuse and stalkers was making her feel uncomfortable.

LINE UP 1986

Toby walked into the playground, his head hung low. He stared aimlessly into the distance, his eyes cold and sad. He almost dragged his feet whilst his shoulders slumped heavily towards the ground. The teacher rang the bell and all the children ran obediently into their class lines, but Toby just stood there almost fixed to the spot. His eyes seemed to look straight through the floor.

'Hurry up boy!' yelled Mr Harris the head teacher. Toby ignored the command. It was as if he was in another world.

'I SAID HURRY UP BOY!'

Toby remained still. Mr Harris was furious. He ushered the lines of children into the school, line by line. Some of the boys pointed at Toby, sniggering amongst themselves. They knew he was in big trouble now.

After all the lines of children had snaked their way into the school, Mr Harris approached Toby. He was not known for his caring nature to say the least and he had interpreted Toby's refusal to move as insolence.

'How dare you ignore me boy!' he bellowed in Toby's face. Mr Harris's eyes were bulging, enraged with being ignored by a child. The veins on the side of his forehead looked like blue worms wriggling and writhing under the surface.

Startled by the loud voice, Toby jumped. He looked up wide eyed at the teacher. Almost instantaneously Toby wet himself and then he began to cry. Being shouted at by Mr Harris had triggered something deep inside him. It was the same feeling that he got when his mother screamed at him. Mr Harris was now beyond furious.

'For God's sake boy, you are a mess!'

Toby bolted out of the playground, tears streaming down his face. He ran over the gravel track and through the lanes that ran parallel to his back yard, but he did not run home. He knew that if he did, he would be in even more trouble. He eventually stopped running when his muscles burned, and he could no longer breathe. He slumped under a huge oak tree, hugged his knees to his chest and sobbed uncontrollably.

FEEDBACK 2013

Almost three years had passed since Kira had started her counselling training. It had been an intense three years and as expected some students had dropped out along the way. The whole college thing was now second nature to Kira and she no longer felt nervous. Soon she would be a fully qualified counsellor. Kira was looking forward to graduating and progressing to the next part of her journey. She had wanted to help others ever since going through her own difficulties in life.

Prompt as always, Nancy waltzed into the

room slinging her scarf over her shoulder flamboyantly as she did so. As usual, Michael was not far behind.

'Good morning everyone,' said Nancy with a warm, genuine smile. 'Today during your personal development session, I want you to give each other some constructive feedback. Remember to include positive as well as negative feedback.'

Kira was in Michael's personal development group along with David, Megan, Leanne and Helen. Helen was a teacher who was retraining as a counsellor because she knew that she could not help children properly in her role as a teacher, she just had this natural ability to know how children felt. Helen was natural and grounded.

'OK then guys,' said Michael, 'Today we are going to give each other some feedback so that we can develop our self-awareness and if necessary, change. I want you to be honest with each other, to say how you experience others in the group. Don't be shy, say strengths as well as weaknesses.' Michael looked around the group. He was well aware of the dynamics of the group, who liked who, who clashed with who and who was playing games.

'I'll start, if that's alright with you all,' said Megan. The group nodded in agreement. Kira was eager to hear what Megan thought about her.

'Kira, you are warm and accepting of others. You never judge people and I have really enjoyed working with you. My only criticism would be that you are sometimes a little too trusting, maybe a little naïve.' Kira could not quite believe that Megan thought she was so nice. She felt like a bit of a fraud, as she blushed and thanked Megan for her feedback.

Next it was Helen's turn, 'Well Kira, you are caring, compassionate and very empathic, but I feel that you are not always as genuine with the group as you could be. Almost like you want to portray yourself as a certain person but you are not that person. I don't mean that you are fake, I just think you are sometimes guarded, a bit too private. Does that make sense?'

Kira nodded. She certainly kept a part of herself private from the group. She could not understand why some of the group members shared so much of themselves. She cringed at the way some of the group members spewed every intimate detail of their lives into the personal development sessions.

Overall, Kira was happy with the feedback that she received. She left college that day feeling happy.

GHOST BOY 1987

Miss Hartman, Toby's teacher, was extremely worried about him. Try as she might, she just could not engage him. He spent most of the school day staring into space or rocking back and forth. Occasionally he made strange noises. He held his clenched hands protectively in front of his stomach. His face was always so pale and drawn and dark circles hung under his eyes. He no longer had any friends. The other children had given up on him. Some of the kids teased him because he smelled. They were sick and tired of being kicked or bitten by him.

So, with a heavy heart, Miss Hartman decided to call in the Local Authority's Child Psychologist. She knew that Mrs Gruneberg was a very experienced child psychologist who had worked with troubled children for over twenty years, and she valued her opinion.

The sky was a murky grey and the rain was heavy on the day of Toby's assessment. Miss Hartman greeted Mrs Gruneberg and gave her an update on Toby. Mrs Gruneberg looked very official with her grey pinstripe suit and leather briefcase. The buzzer sounded and the children milled into the classroom. Mrs Gruneberg sat at the back of the classroom - the best place to get a good view of Toby.

Heavy rain lashed against the windowpanes. Toby stared, transfixed at the rain drops that weaved their way down the glass. He was there but he wasn't there. He ignored Miss Hartman's request to get his pencil case out or to get his book out of his tray. It was almost as if could not hear what she was saying. Some of the children noticed Toby's lack of response, others just thought that Toby was being naughty and was ignoring Miss Hartman on purpose. Conner Davey, the class clown, had nick named Toby 'Ghost Boy' when the teachers were not around. It was a good way to describe him, if not a little cruel. The name had begun to stick and even some of the staff referred to Toby as Ghostie in the safe confines of the staffroom, much to Miss Hartman's dislike.

The rain stopped as quickly as it had started. Within minutes, yellow sunshine filled the room and the energy changed. Little Sally Davies pointed out of the window and exclaimed excitedly:

'Miss Hartman! Look! A double rainbow!'

Before Miss Hartman could respond, at least twenty children had clambered over to the window to get a better look.

'Woooah! It's a double rainbow. How cool is that?' said Adam.

Miss Hartman observed her class. It was a sad sight really; almost every child in the class was in awe of the beautiful rainbow, every child except Toby. Toby was now under the table, humming to himself, rocking backwards and forwards with his thumb wedged firmly in his mouth. He was totally oblivious to the rainbow.

Mrs Gruneberg observed Toby closely. Every few minutes she scribbled in her leather notebook then glanced up again. At the end of the lesson, when all the children had gone out to play, Mrs Gruneberg spoke with Miss Hartman.

'Toby is severely emotionally disturbed. He is displaying incredibly challenging behaviour. Sadly, I think he will have to leave mainstream school. You just cannot cope with him here. He is not getting any work done. I will write an official report but basically my recommendation will be that he goes to Shady View House.'

Even though she was not surprised by the decision, Miss Hartman's heart sank, and tears filled her eyes. Shady View House was the local pupil referral unit, the school for children with emotional and behavioural difficulties. The locals called it '*the sink*' because the only way was down. She averted her gaze from Mrs Gruneberg, willing the tears to disappear. She knew that the boys who went to Shady View House never returned to mainstream school. They became social outcasts who often went on to engage in anti-social behaviour. She had seen it too many times, it was almost as if the rejection from mainstream school caused them to live up to the label of 'naughty' or 'misfit'. She knew that there was nothing she could do to save Toby though, the educational system was too strong for her to tackle. The system had failed Toby, writing him off as unmanageable at just seven years of age, but Miss Hartman knew that underneath the bad behaviour, the physical aggression and the disobedience, there was an incredibly sad and scared little boy.

FULLY QUALIFIED

Kira could not quite believe that the last day of college had finally arrived. She felt relieved, sad and excited all at the same time. She had met some wonderful people but now it was time to start the next chapter of her life as a counsellor. For the final time, Nancy and Michael walked into the room. Nancy paused and smiled before talking,

'Well today is your last day as students. I'm thrilled to say that you have all passed the course and are now ready to practise your skills. I am confident that you will all make wonderful counsellors. I would trust you to counsel my best friend,' she said with a proud glint in her eye.

'We have written you each a letter,' said Michael.

Kira opened hers wondering what it would say:

Dear Kira,
You have worked extremely hard over the last three years. Your assignments have always been excellent. You have been an asset to the group, and it has been a pleasure teaching you and watching you grow. Keep yourself safe, trust, but do not be too trusting. Shine in all you do,
warmest wishes,
Michael.

Kira felt herself blush. She caught Michael's eye and mouthed the words thank you. She had always had a soft spot for Michael.

The day seemed to go so quickly. They ended their final day with a celebratory buffet and a glass each of champagne which of course David had provided. Kira looked around the room at her peers. She observed as they hugged, shed tears, and said their goodbyes. Kira did not like endings, they unsettled her. She could not face saying goodbye to her classmates. When no one else was looking she decided to slip away quietly so she could go home unnoticed without saying goodbye to anyone.

MAN HANDLED 1988

The sky was a dull, heavy grey, much like Toby's mood. The day had arrived for him to start his new school and he was dreading it. He watched through his window as a taxi pulled up outside his house. The horn tooted almost cheerfully. Toby froze. He felt the panic rise within him. It started in his feet then flooded through his system reaching his face and making it difficult for him to breathe. He really did not want to go to Shady View House. He had heard the boys on his estate talk about it. It sounded horrendous.

'Please don't make me go there, Mam,' he begged. His mother picked him up from the ground and dug her fingers into his tiny rib cage. Toby gritted his teeth. He knew that crying out would get him into even more trouble with her. She looked him in the eyes and squeezed as hard as she could. Toby heard an almighty pop. She quickly released her grip, realising that she had broken another rib. The sharp pain that he had felt just minutes before was now replaced with an agonising burning sensation. He could not sit or stand straight, and it was difficult to breathe. She just looked at him and shook her head.

'Taxi's here,' she snarled. Toby knew that it was pointless pleading with her, so he grabbed his rucksack and limped to the door with his elbow supporting his fractured rib. She smiled smugly to herself and uttered,

'That'll teach the little shit to misbehave.' She waved to him from the window, but her smile was one of utter contempt.

Shirley, the taxi escort, had curly red hair and kind sparkly eyes. She jumped out of the taxi and put her hand up to high five Toby, but he recoiled. She opened the taxi door for him, and he clambered in with tears staining his little face. Shirley had been driving kids to Shady View for donkey's years. She knew that although they all acted like they did not care, beneath all the bravado, most were petrified, and so she tried to put Toby at ease.

‘Don't worry little fella, you'll soon get used to Shady View House. It’s not as bad as people make out. There is no need to be scared,’ she said soothingly.

Toby sat in the back of the taxi sobbing silently. Shirley had no idea what he was really crying about.

KIRA'S INTERVIEW 2016

Three years had passed since Kira had left college and after months of trying, she had finally secured an interview for a hospital post. She sat in the interview room at Mount Heath Hospital and tried to conceal her nerves. Opposite her sat two friendly faced forty somethings, one blonde and one brunette.

'Tell us a bit about yourself and your experience in psychotherapy, Kira,' said the blonde lady.

'Well, I qualified from West Trinity University three years ago and I've been working for a local GP's practice ever since then. A lot of my work has been with clients who have depression and anxiety, but I have done quite a bit of training on trauma too.'

'Why do you want to work in a hospital setting Kira?' asked the dark-haired lady.

'Well, if I'm honest, I want more of a challenge. I want to work with clients who need more in-depth psychological support than just listening therapy,' said Kira confidently. The brunette nodded and smiled.

'Are you happy to work with clients who have been sectioned and spent time in hospital? Do you feel confident enough to work with people who have suffered serious trauma? This work is particularly challenging Kira... we would not want to employ you unless you fully understand the nature of the work,' said the blonde.

Kira felt the blood drain from her face and her hands felt clammy. She thought for a moment or so before responding.

'I'm fully aware of the type of work I would be expected to do. I feel confident enough to take on more complex cases. I am sure that with good supervision I will be able to do this role. I have a lot to offer and I have been highly successful with the clients I've worked with so far. I'm ready for this next chapter.'

This however was not strictly true. Kira felt

apprehensive about this new position and had no idea if she was experienced enough to do it justice. She wondered whether she would be out of her depth. These new clients sounded quite difficult and Kira felt anxious.

The two forty somethings looked at each other. Then the blonde lady smiled warmly,

'We'd like to offer you the job Kira. Congratulations! I think you are just who we are looking for.' She held her hand out for Kira to shake.

Kira smiled and shook their hands, now feeling more composed. As she stood up to leave the room, the dark-haired lady added,

'By the way, I think it's helpful if you think of your clients as patients and not clients in this setting Kira.'

Kira nodded, smiled, and left the room.

STRANGE EPISODES 1988

Toby was slowly getting used to Shady View House. He was getting used to the monotonous and rigid daily routines. He missed the familiarity of his old school - the classroom and the playground. Most of all though, he yearned for Miss Hartman's warm smile and gentle touch- he missed being treated as a little boy. At Shady View House the teachers just barked orders at him. The other boys were all weirdos. There was Simon who smeared his own faeces over the toilet walls at least once a week and when he was not doing that, he was pelting wet toilet roll at the ceiling. Then there was Harrison who could hardly speak for twitching and stuttering. He could barely string a sentence together and when he eventually did speak his whole body would jerk. Then there was Ruben who kicked everything in sight. He once kicked a brick wall so hard that he fractured his foot and was on crutches for three months. He even kicked the nurse who did his X- ray at the hospital. Finally, there was Bryson who ate everything in sight, including the crayons and the toilet soap, then walked around frothing at the mouth. Toby had no friends at all here. He did not fit in. He saw them all as freaks.

Most of the staff were control freaks who disliked children. They had ended up at Shady View House because they could not find jobs in mainstream schools. Toby detested most of the staff. They treated him like dirt, and the only teacher he liked was the Irish one. Mr O'Sullivan or Sully, as the kids liked to call him, was boyish and funny. He always treated Toby with respect, even when he had been naughty, but he was also very straight talking. Toby had seen him smoking whilst on his tea break and he had also overheard him swearing in the staff room. Toby could relate to him.

One Tuesday during an English lesson Mr O'Sullivan noticed that there was something wrong with Toby. He looked like he was having some sort of seizure. His eyeballs rolled up into his head and his face went deathly pale. Mr O'Sullivan sat down next to Toby and he gently touched his arm,

'Hey buddy, you OK?' Toby remained silent. After a few moments Toby was back in the room. He looked vaguely at Mr O'Sullivan wondering why he was looking at him so intently. Mr O'Sullivan asked again, 'Are you OK Toby?' Toby nodded. He had no idea what Sully was talking about. These absences began to occur more frequently, and the staff grew increasingly concerned.

The staff at Shady View House called his mother in and insisted he was taken to a neurologist. Mr O'Sullivan carefully explained the situation to Toby's mother.

'Mrs Phoenix, I think that young Toby might be having some sort of fits. He just goes kind of strange. He goes pale, his eyes roll up into his head and he is hard to reach. He needs to be medically assessed,' said Mr O'Sullivan in his boyish Irish accent.

Mrs Phoenix placed her arms on her son's shoulders.

'Oh, you poor thing,' she said, devoid of any real emotion, 'don't worry, I'll sort you out.' She knew exactly how to behave in front of the teachers and staff. She didn't want the social sniffing around and taking her boy away from her. He was especially useful around the house. He put all the bins out, he did the vacuuming and the cooking, and he ran all her errands. Most of all though, her male friends enjoyed having his company in the bedroom at night…….

Mrs Phoenix took Toby to the doctor, she even took the neurology appointment letter to the school to show Mr O'Sullivan. However, Mrs Phoenix never actually took Toby to the hospital. She knew if she did then they would discover the old fractures on his skull.

KIRA MEETS TOBY 2016

Kira pulled into Mount Heath Hospital car park. She drove over the speed bumps and turned left into the multi- story car park. She searched for her name in the staff section, spotted 'Devlin' and parked her car. As always, she was dressed immaculately, and her long shiny blonde hair glistened in the morning sun. She headed towards the sprawling concrete building.

The hospital was a busy hive even at nine a.m. Patients in pyjamas congregated around the main entrance, smoking, and chatting. Kira entered the building through the sliding glass doors. Porters pushed patients on wide trolley beds down the long corridor. A group of young trainee nurses stood chatting in an alcove and visitors made their way to the wards. The smell of lemon disinfectant and fresh laundry filled the air. Kira walked down the never-ending corridor until she reached the Mental Health Suite. She confidently pressed the keypad and the double doors quietly slid open. She subconsciously checked out her appearance in the glass. The glass was tinted so that outsiders could not see in. She unlocked her room and pressed the remote-control blinds open and made herself an espresso whilst her laptop initiated. She looked at her list for the day and her mood lifted when she saw that she had a new patient. She liked the challenge of a new patient. The early counselling relationship was always so interesting, so fresh, and full of hope. She preferred the start of the counselling relationship, as usually once the counselling relationship progressed, things became more complicated. She glanced over the new patient's referral notes. Toby Phoenix, male, thirty-six years old, history of childhood abuse and neglect, numerous suicide attempts, drug and alcohol misuse, panic attacks, depression, anger issues and frequent hospitalisations. She curled her bottom lip. Nothing out of the ordinary here, and nothing she had not seen before she thought.

Kira no longer felt nervous when meeting new patients, instead she was confident and self-assured. The days of feeling petrified by the thought of a new patient were long gone. She was now far more automatic in her approach. She did not have to think about how to discuss the confidentiality issues or how to explain the contract with patients. She no longer worried about what the patient thought of her, she could just be herself. She tapped her pen against her lip as she scanned the referral notes, whilst mentally carrying out a risk assessment. Her thoughts were disturbed by someone knocking the door. Before Kira had time to say come in, Anne, the secretary had popped her head around the door. Anne reminded Kira of a field mouse. She was meek and always scurrying around the corridors.

'Good Morning Kira,' Anne said smiling, 'your new patient has arrived. Shall I send him in?'

Kira nodded, trying to hide her annoyance that he had arrived early. She had not finished skim reading his notes. Kira remained seated as her patient entered the room. She gestured for him to take a seat.

'Hi,' she said gently, 'my name is Kira and I'm a psychotherapist here at Mount Heath Hospital.'

The man sitting opposite her extended his hand but offered no eye contact.

‘My name is Toby,’ he said quietly.

Toby was six foot. He had attractive green eyes that were flooded with sadness, his skin was rugged, weathered even. His wavy hair revealed a certain vulnerability, the curliness reminded Kira of the first curls that often appear on a new-born baby's head. He was very natural looking. That is the only way Kira could describe him. He was still a young man but the crow's feet around his eyes, revealed that he had frowned a lot. Kira was struck by the mismatch between his physical and emotional state. Physically, he was strong. His broad shoulders and muscular form were evident even through his loose shirt, but emotionally he was very fragile, he looked like a broken man.

Kira tried to put Toby at ease. She knew that she had to get this first session right or Toby may never come back again. She needed to develop a rapport with him. She explained a bit about how the therapy would work. She went through the contract and discussed confidentiality. Toby did not really seem to engage, instead he sat with his body hunched forward, his head resting on his palm. He avoided Kira's gaze. His legs were crossed, and the foot which was off the ground tapped fervently in the air. Kira made a mental note of his presentation as she talked. She observed that he constantly peeled the skin off around his thumbs, that he cracked his knuckles impulsively, that he only used the upper quadrant of his chest to breathe, and that his rate of breathing was fast. He was clearly anxious and uncomfortable.

'So, Toby, can you tell me what it is you hope to get out of counselling? What's brought you here?'

Toby sat silently for quite a while. Kira knew he was thinking and needed time to think about his answer.

'Take your time,' she said patiently.

Toby looked up at her for the first time since entering the room. He was hesitant,

'I want to find out if I'm really a monster capable of doing the awful things that I fantasise about,' he said flatly.

Kira glanced at the clock to find that the hour was almost up. She knew that she could not possibly explore what Toby had just said right now. There was no time and it would be wrong to get him to open up and then send him home. That would leave him exposed and vulnerable.

'OK,' said Kira smiling kindly, 'you would like to explore who you are and what you are capable of. I am aware that our hour is nearly up so maybe we could pick up from here next session? Do you think you will be able to work with me?'

Toby nodded. He liked her… she made him feel the way that Miss Hartman had done all those years ago. Not many people in his life had made him feel like that.

TOBY'S DAD

Toby turned up for his weekly counselling session and he seemed a bit more relaxed. He sat with his legs apart and his arms uncrossed. Kira assessed the situation. Toby was very gradually coming out of his shell. If she misjudged the situation, she could cause him to retreat. She desperately wanted to ask him why he thought he was a monster and what exactly were these 'awful things' that he fantasised about. But she resisted. She knew that Toby needed to go at his own pace and if she rushed him, she could cause a rupture in their relationship. She could lose him. Kira decided to play it safe. She asked a broad question which invited Toby to talk but also allowed him total control over what he revealed.

'Tell me about yourself Toby.'

Toby looked out through the window, he seemed to be focusing on the birds in the trees. However, Kira knew not to disturb his thoughts, he was processing what she had said and was thinking about his answer.

'Take your time,' Kira said softly.

Toby started talking but his gaze remained on the birds.

'There's not much to tell really. I was brought up on Bramwell Council Estate. I've got six brothers and sisters. My father died when I was five, he hung himself in the woods. I was a little bastard in school. The teachers could not control me, so I got sent to Shady View House when I was seven. When I left there aged sixteen, I did some time inside, petty stuff really, you know… burglaries, drugs, fights. That's me really.'

Kira felt sad, although she already knew most of Toby's history the thought of him being five when his Dad died upset her. She made a mental note about him being emotionally detached whilst talking about his life. He talked about traumatic events in the same way someone else would read out a shopping list. Was he consciously minimising what had happened in his life? Was it a coping mechanism? He did not get emotionally aroused at all. It was as though he were talking about somebody else's life.

Kira was used to multi-tasking when working with patients. There was an art to listening to a patient's story, whilst simultaneously assessing them and also keeping her own emotional reactions in check. Kira considered her response and decided to focus on the death of his father. A hypothesis had started to form at the back of her mind, maybe Toby had been traumatised by the loss of his father and not dealt with his grief. This had led on to a spiral of events which had almost destroyed Toby. Kira knew that she needed to get Toby to engage with his emotions surrounding his father's death, but she also knew not to assume anything about Toby's relationship with his father. He may have hated him or been abused by him.

'So, your father died suddenly when you were five. What was that like for you?' asked Kira.

Something in Toby's face changed, just subtly, but other than that, there was no emotion.

'It broke my heart. He was my hero.'

Toby's words did not match his voice, he seemed devoid of any emotion and this was slightly unsettling to Kira. He was so detached from himself. Kira wanted to help him to get in touch with the feelings that he had pushed down.

'Toby, your father's death has had a big impact on you and you clearly loved him. How would you feel about doing an exercise to help you to get in touch with the emotions you felt then and now?' asked Kira.

Toby often felt numb and privately thought that Kira's idea was pointless but decided to give it a try. Kira asked Toby to close his eyes, and she got him to take some deep breaths and put him in a meditative state. Softly, she asked him to imagine that his father was there sitting in the room with him. She carefully monitored his responses.

'What do you want to say to your father Toby?'

Toby began talking. 'I want to tell him…'

Kira gently interrupted him. 'Talk directly to your father Toby. Use his name.'

Toby felt silly but gave it a go.

'Dad, I have really missed you. There are so many things that I want to tell you. I am hoping to turn my life around and make you proud of me.'

Kira encouraged Toby to keep going. Toby talked to his Dad like this for over half an hour. Suddenly though, Toby's mood changed, and he became tense, angry. Kira gently encouraged Toby to keep going.

‘Why did you go Dad? Why did you leave me? How could you leave me with that cruel bitch!?’ Toby’s faced was strained as if he was holding back tears, and the blood had drained from his face. He was now breathing rapidly; this was the first time that Kira had seen any emotion rise to the surface. Toby was clearly angry with his father for dying and leaving him alone with his mother.

Kira glanced at her watch. The session was coming to an end. She desperately wanted to know about 'the bitch', but she knew that she had to bring the session to a close and ensure Toby was safe enough to leave the session.

‘Toby, when you are ready, open your eyes and gently bring your attention back to the room.’ Kira had noticed that his respiratory rate had increased. Physiologically he was aroused. ‘Toby, thank you for doing that exercise. How did it feel?’

‘It felt like my Dad was in the room with me. It felt real.’

Kira spent the next ten minutes doing some breathing exercises with Toby to relax him. Then she talked to Toby about his plans for the rest of the week and when she was sure that he was OK, she let him leave the room.

SUPERVISION

Every month Kira, like all counsellors, had to have supervision to make sure that she was working safely. Kira had been using Faye as a supervisor for the past few years. Faye ran her practice from home, dividing her time between counselling and supervising. Kira walked hurriedly up the street to Faye's house. She wrapped her wool coat tightly around her body, protecting herself from the cold winter's air. She frowned slightly as the icy wind blew hard into her face. She arrived at fifteen Cathedral Place, the home of her supervisor. As she walked down the driveway, she realised that she felt slightly apprehensive, but she did not know why. She stopped as she got to the front door. There was something inviting about the porch, with its spider plants and wind chimes. Kira liked its character and took a moment to appreciate it before she gently tapped the brass knocker. Almost instantly, the door opened, and Faye appeared.

Faye was an attractive lady in her early sixties. She wore a long smock top that reminded Kira of her old art teacher at school and her wrists were adorned with various bangles that jangled as she walked, whilst her wavy grey hair hung loosely on her shoulders.

'Come on in,' she said to Kira, smiling effortlessly. Kira followed Faye through to the back room. 'Well then,' said Faye, 'how are you and what do you want to explore today in supervision?'

Kira took a deep breath in. She did not really know where to start.

'OK, so I'd like to talk about a new patient called Toby. Toby has been referred to the hospital by his doctor. He was badly abused as a child. His mother mistreated him, no, she hated him if truth be told. His Dad died when he was only five and he has not dealt with the loss. He was a difficult child, expelled from school and eventually he got into trouble with the police.'

Faye nodded, occasionally jotting down some notes.

'So, what does he want to achieve from counselling?' she probed.

'Well he believes he is some sort of monster, but we haven't really gotten any further than that,' Kira paused and looked down at the ground.

'What is it you want to discuss Kira? How do you feel when you're in the room with him?' Faye asked.

'Well that's just it,' said Kira, 'he seems so normal. I mean he's a little guarded and doesn't show much emotion but other than that he seems OK. He's a little cold, I guess, but he may just be nervous.'

'OK,' said Faye, 'it sounds like you are saying you would expect him to be more affected by his upbringing and the trauma, yet he's quite well adjusted.'

'Yes, that's exactly it,' said Kira, 'he's quite likeable actually.'

'Well that's very possible Kira, people are resilient. It's quite possible that he has survived the years of abuse and come out the other side,' said Faye. There was a momentary silence that hung between them. Then Faye spoke again.

'Of course, I don't need to tell you that there is a possibility that the years of abuse have had detrimental side effects. If he has never been shown love and affection, he might not be capable of warmth. We learn empathy when we are children, we are not born with it. He could have a psychopathic personality. He may be incapable of feeling empathy or remorse. Psychopaths are very clever at passing as normal and they are notoriously difficult to spot.'

Kira's face paled, and she felt quite uncomfortable. She decided to try and steer the conversation away from all this talk of psychopaths.

'So, what's the way forward with Toby?' asked Kira.

'Well I believe you need to explore this self-concept of his. Who is the monster? Why is Toby so fearful of this monster within him? Ask him what the monster is capable of doing.'

Kira scribbled the questions into her notebook. She felt nervous about her next counselling session with Toby, nervous about what may be revealed.

A CHANCE ENCOUNTER

Kira scraped back her long blond hair and twisted it into a high ponytail, it made her look younger and even more attractive than normal. She pulled on her running shorts, threw on a vest and grabbed a bottle of water from the large American fridge that took pride of place in her kitchen.

Kira loved running and ran most mornings. Running was her therapy, it helped her to get out of her head for a while. She jogged gently through the back streets and into her local park. She loved Golden Grove Park, it was so huge that she could get lost in it. She ran under the tall fir trees and followed the stream as it weaved its way through the woods. It did not take long before she was in the zone and her breathing and strides were in sync.

After a while, she came to a clearing. She bent over to catch her breath resting her hands on her knees. As she looked up, her heart missed a beat. On the opposite side of the park was Toby. She kept her gaze firmly on him, but he did not look over. Kira could not work out whether Toby had seen her but was pretending not to have, or whether he genuinely had not seen her. Either way, she felt slightly uncomfortable about the encounter. Why had Toby seemed to avoid her gaze? She tried to put these thoughts to the back of her mind, but they lingered heavily. She wiped the sweat from her brow, turned hastily and ran back home.

As soon as Kira got home, she felt more relaxed and reflected on the brief encounter in the park. Counsellors are not allowed to have contact with patients outside of the allocated hour, but it was a chance encounter, a mere coincidence. It was not like they had agreed to meet in the park. They had not even spoken, but still, the incident niggled away at Kira. She could not put her finger on this feeling of unease. She made herself a pot of tea and sat at the table. She decided that she was being silly, after all no harm had been done. She also decided not to mention the park incident to Toby unless, of course, he brought the subject up in his next session.

THE MONSTER WITHIN

Toby's weekly counselling sessions seemed to roll around quicker each week. He wrapped his knuckles on Kira's door but entered without waiting for an answer. Kira had her back to Toby when he entered the room. Her smart trouser suit fitted her like a glove; teamed with heels and a silver bracelet she looked really smart. Toby appeared to do a double take when she turned to face him and Kira felt herself blush. She had been trained to control her emotions and monitor her body language, but she could not control physiological reactions like blushing.

Kira looked down momentarily then composed herself. She wondered whether Toby would mention the park incident.

'Hi Toby, how was your week?' Kira asked smiling gently.

Toby was more at ease with her now. He smiled warmly back at her as he sat down.

'It's been pretty routine really. I haven't done that much. I've taken my dog out for walks in the park, watched a few films, done some rock climbing, nothing too exciting.'

Kira was relieved that Toby was not hiding the fact that he had been at the park, although she had not noticed a dog with him. She decided not to dwell on this though. Toby looked at her, expecting her to ask another question.

Kira felt that the time was right to revisit that first session. She had been seeing Toby for about six months now. It had taken that long for her to build a trusting relationship with him. She knew she needed to tread extremely carefully. They had spent the last six months processing Toby's grief and exploring his childhood.

'Toby, can we review our sessions? Asked Kira.

Toby nodded. He seemed comfortable with this suggestion.

'At the end of the first session you said that you believed you were some sort of monster and that you had some monstrous thoughts. What did you mean by that?'

Kira let the question hang in the air. The silence grew louder, but Kira did not fill it. Toby shifted his weight in the armchair, then slowly began to speak.

'In the small hours of the morning, when I cannot sleep, my thoughts go back to my childhood. I think of my mother... and the things she did to me... and the things that she made me do to others. I just feel such hatred.' Toby's fists tightened, and his breathing quickened. This was the biggest reaction that Kira had seen in Toby to date. She quickly assessed the situation. Toby was getting angry and she did not know where it would stop. She wondered whether she was safe. She glanced at the panic button on the windowsill and felt reassured. In that split second, she decided to take a risk and let Toby continue.

'When I was a kid, I thought it was normal. I thought that all mothers were like mine. I thought that all mothers hit their kids and called them evil little bastards. I mean you take your childhood for granted, don't you? You think that your life is normal. As I got into my early teens, I realised that my life was far from normal. I realised that it was not me that was evil, it was her. When I think about her now, well I…' Toby trailed off.

'What happens when you think about her now

Toby?' Kira asked.

Toby hesitated, then looked Kira directly in the eyes and uttered, 'I just want to kill her.'

The words hung in the room like a vile stench. Kira knew that she needed to say something. She decided to reflect his words back to him.

'You just want to kill her.'

Now it was Kira's breathing that quickened. She was unsure of what to do or say next, so she said nothing. Toby's jaw was clenched and there were beads of sweat on his temples.

'I sometimes think about wrapping my hands around that bitch's neck and squeezing the living daylights out of the fucking whore!'

Toby searched Kira's face for a response. Kira decided to focus on Toby's feelings rather than the fact he had just admitted to wanting to murder his mother.

'You want her to pay for what she did. You want her to feel desperate like you felt. You feel angry and you want revenge. You want her to suffer like you did. I understand why you feel this way. Anyone in your position might feel the same.' Kira wanted to normalise his anger at the way he had been treated as a child.

Toby felt somewhat relieved. He began to relax, and he began to really trust Kira.

'The thing is, I don't know whether these are just thoughts or whether I really am capable of killing another human being. What if I really am a monster, Kira? I want to do it so much. I dream about killing her. It's more than a dream, it's a fantasy.'

'So, you're worried that you are actually capable of killing? You believe that you may be a monster.'

'I know that I'm capable of it, I've fantasised about it often enough.'

Kira let the words hang like a veil between them. She processed what he was saying. She wanted to tell him that everything would be OK. When she looked at him all she could see was the vulnerable little boy within him, but she was unnerved by the potential killer that sat opposite her. She wanted to help him but feared that he was already too damaged. There was a coldness to him. Was he really capable of killing his own mother? Kira glanced at the clock, the hour was almost up, and she had another patient waiting outside her room.

'Toby, we'll have to pick this back up next week. Thank you for being so brave and so honest. That must have been extremely difficult for you.'

Toby nodded and half smiled at her. He looked drained. They sat in silence for a little while then Kira broke the silence.

'Do you have any plans this week, Toby?'

asked Kira. She wanted to bring Toby back into the present moment. She also wanted to make sure he had no plans to act out his fantasies.

'I'm going to an old friend's funeral on Tuesday.'

'I am sorry for your loss,' said Kira.

'Thanks, Duffy was a mate from the Bramwell Estate. He died of a drug overdose. I'm not surprised really, he was mad. On a more positive note, I am going rock climbing on Friday.'

Toby loved climbing. Scaling the rocks helped him to forget real life and made him feel strong and free. He loved the adrenalin rush that he got from it and it was one of the only times he felt fully alive.

Kira smiled, satisfied that Toby was OK.

'Well enjoy your climb, I'll see you next week.'

FRIEND REQUEST

Kira sat at the breakfast bar in her kitchen. Her kitchen reflected her personality. It was sleek, organised, and attractive. An expensive coffee machine whirred quietly in the background. Kira sat on the backless chrome stool and flipped open her glossy red laptop. She liked to browse the internet to relax. Just like running, the internet helped her to escape her thoughts. Sometimes she needed to escape from her patients who took up too much headspace.

Kira flitted from site to site enjoying the distraction of the internet. Suddenly, the notification tab flashed. Kira felt slightly annoyed by this interruption. She could see that it was a Facebook notification.

During her training Kira had been warned about using Facebook. In fact, Nancy had categorically told the students that they should not use Facebook or any other social networking sites. Kira remembered feeling annoyed at being dictated to by Nancy. She was a grown adult, and no one was going to tell her that she could not use Facebook. That break time, the students had chatted about Nancy's advice. Kira remembered that some of the students thought that Facebook was a bad idea (notably David and Megan). The majority had concluded that if it was used sensibly there was no real harm in it. It was all about boundaries really. Kira had decided that she would use Facebook but never mention her clients or her work online. She was happy with that.

Kira clicked on the notification tab. She had a friend request. Intrigued, she clicked on the request. Toby's face filled the screen. Toby had sent her a friend request! She felt slightly annoyed that he had imposed on her private life but slightly excited too. There was no escaping the fact that Toby was very handsome. He was so rugged. Kira scanned his profile picture. It was him to a tee, unassuming and self-conscious. The photo had obviously been taken by someone else. Toby was glancing away from the camera. He had that distant look in his eyes that he often seemed to wear. Kira knew that she could not possibly accept a friend request from a patient, the boundary issues were far too complex. She hovered the mouse over the ‘delete request’ button but something stopped her from pressing it. Something at the back of her mind prevented her from pressing ignore. Kira knew that she would have to take it to supervision though, she would have to tell Faye about Toby’s friend request.

MURDEROUS THOUGHTS

Kira was not in the mood for her monthly supervision session, but it was not a choice, so Kira drove the familiar route to Faye's house. Before long she reached Cathedral Place and she parked the car half up on the pavement as the street was quite narrow. Kira sensed the neighbours watching her as she walked up the street towards Faye's house. She wondered what they thought of her. Did they think she was a client? Did they think that she had come for a counselling session? Of course, Faye could never tell them because she was bound by the confidentiality clause. Kira knocked on the door and Faye appeared. Faye wore an emerald green smock dress that floated behind her as she walked. Her hair seemed more tousled each time Kira saw her, and her eyes twinkled as she greeted Kira.

'Come on in, take a seat.'

Kira sat opposite her and waited for Faye to speak first.

'So, what do you want to explore today Kira?'

Kira knew that she had to talk about Toby's desire to kill his mother. She looked down at her notebook and tried to be quite casual about Toby's admission.

'Well I'd like to discuss Toby. We explored his feelings about being a monster. We unpicked what it meant to him. He said that he has monstrous thoughts. He thinks about killing his mother.'

Faye looked a bit surprised. 'Do you believe he is capable of murder Kira?'

Kira did not know what she believed. The one thing that she did know was that Toby would be happier if his mother was dead.

'I don't think he would actually kill her Faye. I think that he is trying to get justice in his head for the wrongs she did to him.'

Faye scribbled in her notepad documenting Kira's concerns. Then she looked up and said,

'Kira, we have to balance Toby's right to confidentiality with the duty of care that we have to others. You need to assess whether Toby is just fantasising about killing his mother or whether he is serious about it. Keep an eye on the situation. If he makes any concrete plans, you will have to contact the police.' Kira nodded in agreement but hoped that Toby was just venting.

'Is there anything else you want to discuss about Toby Kira?'

For a second Kira decided not to mention the friend request on Facebook but she knew that she had to. After all, she could not keep secrets from her supervisor. Kira felt a bit awkward as she shifted her weight on the chair.

'Toby has sent me a friend request on Facebook, I have ignored it of course but I just thought I should mention it.'

Kira knew that her face was reddening and that she was getting flustered. A red mottled rash spread upwards from her cleavage to her neck. She was annoyed with herself for allowing her emotions to show so readily. Faye studied Kira and saw that Kira looked a bit uncomfortable and Faye wondered why.

'Kira, what does this mean to you? How are you interpreting this request?'

Kira flushed again. Damn you she said to herself. She really had not wanted to get into this.

'Well, I think it's just a case of Toby not really understanding that I cannot have him as a friend. Maybe I have not made the counselling relationship clear enough to him. Maybe I need to be more explicit with him about the nature of our relationship.'

Faye looked at the red rash that was appearing on Kira's chest. She noted how anxious Kira appeared.

'Kira, what is it that you are so uncomfortable about? Why are you so tense? What is going on for you?'

Kira was a bit taken aback. She had not realised that she was displaying her discomfort like a badge.

'Well, I guess if I'm completely honest I think that maybe Toby is… I think that Toby may... I think that maybe Toby is attracted to me.'

Kira felt a little bit big headed saying this, but she knew that she had to be honest in supervision about her relationship with her patients. Faye was not surprised. She had come across this many time before. It was not at all uncommon for a patient to idolise their counsellor, or even to become infatuated or fall in love with them. After all, Kira was an attractive woman, even though she seemed largely unaware of her effect on men.

'How do you feel about Toby Kira?' asked Faye. Kira paused for a moment, because she liked to consider what she was going to stay before speaking.

'Well, mostly I like him, but sometimes he scares me, our relationship scares me.'

'In what way?'

'He is so intense. Sometimes I wonder if he is capable of some of the things that he fantasises about, but I want to keep working with him. Too many people in the past have let him down, his mother, his teachers, his youth workers, his probation officer. I do not want to be another person on that list.'

Faye took a moment to think about the situation. She rested her chin gently on her fist.

'Hmm, this is a difficult one. I think you are going to have to address Toby's feelings towards you for the work to progress. You cannot just pretend it is not happening. This is potentially dangerous ground Kira. How might you go about addressing this issue with Toby, Kira?'

Kira was unsure how to answer. She felt a feeling of dread low down in her gut. What if she was wrong and Toby had no feelings for her? She would then feel so stupid for addressing it with him. Part of her wanted to just ignore it and see how things progressed, but she knew that she had to be ethical and protect Toby. After all, he was vulnerable and if he had developed feelings for her, she could not just sweep it under the carpet.

'I suppose I will start by bringing up the friend request and ask him how he views our relationship. I will be able to see from his body language and facial expression what he really feels.' For a second, Kira contemplated telling Faye that she had seen Toby in the park.

Faye was happy with this answer. She needed to know that Kira was not going to ignore the situation because that could be perceived as encouraging Toby.

'Just one last thing' said Faye, 'You need to remember that you are working with someone who probably doesn't know how to make healthy attachments to others. The likelihood is that he either over attaches or under attaches to others. Explore how he relates to others in his life and remember that we learn secure attachments from our parents Kira. Toby's mother was certainly not a secure base for Toby and his father died when he was at a very pivotal age. Just be careful that Toby does not over attach to you. Make sure that he does not become dependent on you. It's not healthy.'

Kira nodded. She knew that Faye was right and that there was every possibility that Toby was developing an unhealthy obsession with her. She left supervision with a clearer picture of what was happening.

As she walked back to her car, Kira suddenly

froze. From the corner of her eye, she caught a fleeting glimpse of Toby running into the alleyway across the street. At least she was fairly sure that it was Toby as the man had the same build and the same broad shoulders. She quickened her pace so that she could look up the alleyway, but Toby had gone.

STRANGE EPISODES

Kira was quite nervous about addressing the relationship thing with Toby, but she had rehearsed exactly what she was going to say. She scanned her card in the keypad and the double doors opened. To her surprise, Toby was already in the waiting room, and his appointment was not for another thirty minutes. He sat hunched forward with his head in his hands, and he did not look happy. Kira was struck by how handsome he looked. He had a t-shirt and shorts on. His shoulders were broad. He sat with his legs open revealing his strong, muscular thighs. For an instant Kira felt attracted to him but immediately pushed this feeling aside. She knew what was going on. If Toby was attracted to her, she was responding with countertransference. She felt slightly annoyed that Toby was there early. He was again pushing her boundaries but as she wanted to get this difficult conversation out of the way, she called him in early. Toby did not even wait for Kira to sit down before he started talking.

'I need help. I think I am having some strange episodes. I used to get them when I was younger but haven't had them for a while,' he blurted out.

'Tell me about them,' said Kira.

'Well, I looked at my Facebook account yesterday and there were some status updates that I have no recollection of writing. I mean, I have been knocking the Jack Daniels back a bit lately and I haven't exactly been sleeping properly, but I have no memory of writing the last few statuses.'

Kira felt derailed. She had worked herself up to discuss the friend request in today's session, but this new revelation had now thrown a spanner in the works. Toby looked so worried. She knew she had to deal with the issue in front of her, the relationship stuff would have to take a back seat.

'What are you imagining Toby? What do you think is going on?' Kira gently probed.

'Well, maybe I'm going mad. Maybe I'm so damaged that I'm losing the plot.'

Toby glanced up at Kira searching her face for a response. Kira had so much going on in her head. She wondered whether Toby was dissociating, or worse still, maybe he had developed two different personalities? She remembered reading a case study about a woman called Lizzy who had been so abused as a child that she had developed multiple personalities. Strangely, none of them knew each other. It was bizarre. Kira wondered whether Toby was doing things that he did not know he was doing, or could he be taking too many of his sleeping pills and mixing them with Jack Daniels? Or maybe his Facebook account had been hacked?

Kira knew that her response would influence how Toby viewed himself. He trusted her and her perception of him. She smiled warmly at him,

'Toby, you are under a lot of stress. Having counselling opens old wounds up and can make us feel very vulnerable. It can even re-traumatise us. When we are stressed, we do things on autopilot. We do things and don't remember doing them. We have difficulty concentrating and remembering. This is completely normal.'

Toby's face seemed to relax a little but there was still a tiny muscle twitching in his upper jaw, showing that he was still anxious. They spent the rest of the session working on some relaxation exercises and Toby agreed to try and drink less and sleep more. After Toby left the room, Kira searched the internet for ‘absences’. She had a feeling of dread in the pit of her stomach.

THE CEMETERY

Every month, Kira visited Greenfield Cemetery to tend to her parents' grave. She felt better when there were fresh flowers on the grave and she found the cemetery strangely calming. The old cemetery was only a twenty-minute drive from her house, and she enjoyed driving through the narrow country lanes.

She parked her car under some leafy elm trees and drank in the stunning views over the nearby bay. The light glistened on the sea in the distance and the birds chirped in the trees above her. She loved the tranquillity of this place.

Kira opened the boot of her car and took out a bunch of roses, a pair of scissors, a water bottle, and an old cleaning rag. She weaved her way amongst the headstones until she spotted the old familiar family grave. She knelt on the ground in front of the headstone and ran her fingers over the inscriptions on the stone showing her parents' names. She still could not really accept what had happened.

She cleaned the moss off the stone using the old rag. One by one she pulled out the red roses, cutting them diagonally and removing leaves from the bottom of the stems. Routinely, she emptied the pot's slug ridden grimy water and replenished it with clear water from the tap in the field. She placed the roses back in the pot and rearranged them until she was satisfied. Then she sat on her knees and stared at the fresh flowers that rested against the weathered headstone.

She felt completely numb. She had often told her bereavement patients that grief is personal, that it did not matter if they visited cemeteries or not. She had also told them that they did not need to cry to prove they missed their loved ones. However, Kira felt a little uncomfortable about not crying for her parents.

As Kira rearranged the silver sleeping angel ornament on the grave something caught her eye. In the car park across the way, Toby was stepping out of his car. Something stirred inside her. This was all so wrong, but she dismissed the uncomfortable feeling. It was just a coincidence, two grieving people at a cemetery, nothing more, nothing less. Kira hurried back to her car before Toby had time to approach to her. It would have been too awkward.

VALENTINE'S DAY

Kira sat in her kitchen and opened the mail. The local radio station played in the background. They were announcing Valentine messages and playing special Valentine dedications. Kira did not like Valentine's Day, she thought it was an over commercialised waste of money. She sliced up some fresh strawberries, blueberries and a banana and made herself a fruit smoothie. She settled down with her laptop to write up some notes from last week's counselling sessions. Just as she was getting into it, she was disturbed by the intrusive metal clanging of the front door knocker. Someone was keen for her to answer. Kira opened the door, frowning.

'Hiya love, are you Kira Devlin?' asked the man who was standing on her doorstep.

Kira nodded and the man handed her a massive bouquet of flowers adorned with red hearts and twirling ribbons.

'Well, you're a lucky lady then, these are from our luxury range. Somebody obviously thinks a lot of you,' he winked.

Kira looked down at the flowers, then quickly looked up and down the street. Something inside her told her that these were from Toby. She should feel annoyed with him as he was over-stepping another boundary. All she could hear was Nancy's voice in her head,

'Remember, be careful, some clients can push boundaries and get inside your personal world.'

Kira did not feel annoyed though, in fact, in a very strange way she felt flattered. Kira opened the flowers, cut the ends and then placed them in a crystal vase on the table. She wondered whether or not to tell Faye about the flowers as she had no proof that they were from Toby. In fact, they could be from anyone.

TOBY AND LAYLA

Toby had been seeing his girlfriend Layla for about six months. He really liked her but was scared to get too close to her. Layla was a natural beauty with wavy blonde sun-kissed hair and tanned skin. She was petite but looked even more so beside Toby's muscular frame. She was only twenty-five, quite a bit younger than Toby and they made a striking couple.

Layla and Toby were sleeping, bodies entwined. Layla's back faced Toby. His forearm rested loosely around Layla's chest. Gradually, Toby became restless, extremely restless. Layla awoke. Toby tossed his head from side to side and started muttering. Layla could not quite make out what Toby was saying. She could feel his body tense and his breathing quicken. Then, he began to sweat profusely. Layla tried to move to wake him up, but Toby now had her in an arm-lock. She could not move. By now Toby was shouting.

'NO! NO! PLEASE NO!' Toby pleaded.

He was having another nightmare. Layla tried to wake him up, but she was stuck in his arm-lock.

'Toby! Toby! You are OK. I'm here. It's just a nightmare. It's not real.'

Toby was sleeping too deeply to hear Layla's voice. She used her foot to kick him sharply using the back of her heel. This was enough to jolt Toby out of his nightmare. Toby blinked suddenly awake, beads of sweat peppered his forehead. His eyes were glassy and grey.

'Are you OK honey? You were shouting in your sleep,' said Layla.

Toby got up without answering Layla or even looking at her. She heard him turn the shower on. Toby stood in the shower and turned the cold water on full. He held his head in his hands and cried. Layla felt so sorry for him, he was getting more and more of these nightmares. She quickly stripped the sheets off the bed, not even sure if

Toby knew he had wet the bed.

NIGHT TERRORS

Toby was worried that he may hurt Layla during one of these night terrors. In his next therapy session Toby confided in Kira about the nightmares that were plaguing his sleep.

'I cannot go on like this! They are driving me crazy. Are there any sleeping pills that I can take? I seriously need to get some decent sleep.'

Kira looked at him. His face looked pale and dark shadows hung under his eyes. He looked exhausted and seemed desperate.

'I cannot prescribe drugs for you Toby. You will have to see your doctor about medication.

Psychotherapists are not licensed to prescribe drugs, but we can talk about the nightmares if you like.'

Toby stared at his hands for a while. Kira waited, for it is often in the silent moments of conversations that people find their inner voice.

'I can't remember the nightmare itself. It is the same thing on repeat though. I just remember the ending.'

'Go on,' said Kira.

'Well, I notice my heart beating ten to the dozen and I feel all hot and clammy. I struggle to open my eyes and I try to speak but I can't. It feels like I am awake, but I am totally unable to move. I am paralysed. Then I look down, and on the ground at my feet is my mother with blood oozing out of her head.'

Kira shuddered. It must be awful to have such vivid nightmares. Kira assured Toby that it was normal to have nightmares whilst having therapy.

'When we dredge up old memories, our subconscious needs to process them. Sometimes this results in dreams or nightmares. It is to be expected.'

Kira wondered whether Toby was having seizures in his sleep. It was a possibility, so she gently suggested to Toby to mention the nightmares and sleep paralysis to his doctor.

Toby dutifully took Kira's advice and made an

appointment to see his doctor. He told the doctor about his childhood episodes and the concerns that Mr O'Sullivan had about him when he was a child. He also told the doctor about the bed wetting and said that he thought he could be having absences. Dr Midha was concerned enough to refer Toby to a neurologist to rule out anything organic. The neurologist did an EEG on Toby's brain and took a full medical history. He also did an MRI and CAT scan. As Toby lay in the MRI scanner, his mind flooded with images from his childhood, the beatings, the emotional abuse, the bullying from the other school kids, and the men. He found it impossible to block out these images. It was as if the floodgates had been opened and he could not close them, like Pandora's Box. He tried to focus on his breathing like Kira had taught him, but his mind was in overdrive. He was in a state by the time he eventually got out of the MRI tunnel.

Two weeks later Toby went to the doctors to get his results. The neurology report said that nothing abnormal had been detected on any of the scans or tests. Toby should have felt relieved, but he didn't. He simply wondered what was causing him to have these memory lapses and nightmares, and he began to doubt his own sanity.

END IT OR ELSE

Monthly supervision rolled around so quickly. Kira decided that she would not talk about Toby in supervision today, instead she would focus on a different patient. Faye, however, had other ideas. She had felt quite uncomfortable when Kira had left last month and wanted to ensure that Kira had addressed the friend request issue with Toby.

'So, Kira, let's revisit last month's session. How did things go with Toby?' Kira's stomach lurched. She had hoped to avoid the whole Toby issue today but now she had no choice.

'Well I never got to address the friend request issue because Toby told me he was having blackout episodes and I felt it would have been insensitive. I could not ignore his physical health to address niggles around our relationship, Faye,' said Kira.

Faye nodded but said nothing. Kira wished she knew what Faye was thinking, but Faye held her cards close to her chest. After a while Faye asked,

'Do you have any other concerns about Toby?'

Kira fidgeted with her fingers, and Faye noticed this.

'Well it's probably nothing, but when I left here last month, I thought I saw Toby walking up the alleyway across the road. I am not sure that it was him, but it looked like him. I also saw him at the cemetery when I was tending my parents' grave… but there could have been a valid reason as to why he was there.'

Faye looked directly at Kira, then asked, 'Anything else?' Kira was not sure whether to mention the Valentine flowers, but she knew that she needed to be honest with Faye.

'Look, I have absolutely no evidence for thinking this, but I received a bouquet of flowers on Valentine's Day. There is no one special in my life at the moment, so I'm thinking that maybe Toby sent them. Maybe he thinks this relationship is more than a counselling relationship.'

Faye frowned and looked concerned, 'You know what you have to do right?'

Kira's heart sank. She did not want to finish working with Toby. She honestly believed that she could help him.

'I know it looks bad, but there's just something about him Faye that makes me want to continue working with him. When I look at him, all I can see is the vulnerable little mistreated boy who is crying out to be saved.'

Faye looked at Kira with concern. 'Kira, let me be absolutely straight with you. Toby has not just overstepped a boundary. He is not just pushing his luck. He has become infatuated with you. It sounds like he may even be stalking you! I am gravely concerned for your well-being. If you do not terminate the counselling contract with Toby, then I shall have no other option than to report you to the Counselling Agency.'

Tears welled up in Kira's eyes. She knew that Faye was right and that she could no longer work safely with Toby. She knew that a counselling relationship could never work if someone became obsessed. She also knew that she would have to refer him on to a colleague. Faye got out her notebook and documented everything that they had discussed, and Kira knew there was no going back now.

THE ENDING

Kira had been awake most of the night tossing and turning. She did not know how to end things with Toby, but she knew she had to. It had taken ages for Toby to trust and confide in her and now she could not counsel him anymore. Kira did not know how to start the conversation. Toby came into the room and sat down confidently. He had come such a long way since that first session. He had really started to process his childhood and come to terms with his grief. Kira looked everywhere apart from at Toby. Toby sensed her discomfort. He was quite intuitive.

'Is everything OK Kira? What's wrong?' he asked.

'I have something I need to discuss with you Toby.' She decided to get straight to the point and get it over and done with. 'This is not easy for me to say and I don't think it will be easy for you to hear, I don't think I can work with you anymore. I am going to have to pass you onto one of my colleagues here at the hospital.'

Toby frowned. He looked confused and hurt.

'Is it something I've done? Did I do something wrong? Was it something I said?' he asked.

Kira decided to be honest with him, 'I think that maybe our relationship has overstepped some boundaries. I mean, you have sent me a request on Facebook …' Before Kira could finish, Toby interrupted her,

'I did not! If I did, I certainly don't remember doing so.'

Kira sensed that he was getting angry and knew she needed to calm him down. He cracked each knuckle individually and his face reddened. Kira noticed his jaw tighten.

'You can't do this to me Kira! You can't just open up a can of worms and then leave it with the lid off. I feel totally exposed. I trusted you. I love working with you. I am just starting to make sense of my screwed-up life!'

Kira started to panic a little. He was taking this much worse than she had expected. She glanced at the panic button on the window and momentarily considered pressing it. Just at that moment, a shrill alarm went off, breaking the tension that was palpable in the room. It was the hospital's fire alarm.

Kira escorted Toby out of the nearest exit and joined the other patients and counsellors in the rear car park of the hospital.

'I'm off then, there's no point in me hanging around here,' said Toby.

'Please Toby, don't be hasty. Let's go back inside and discuss this. At least let us end this properly,' Kira pleaded.

But Toby was upset and angry and he had already made up his mind. He stormed off without looking back. Kira had not wanted it to end like this and she genuinely felt really sad. She watched his familiar figure head off into the distance. She felt awful.

MRS PHOENIX

Mrs Phoenix was now in her late seventies, she was overweight and haggard. Her large frame was no longer a threatening presence, more of an empty carcass now. A lifetime of drinking and smoking had left a myriad of deep lines on her wrinkled face. Her expression was frozen into a grumpy scowl, and the corners of her mouth were dragged down. Her chipped teeth were yellow and black in places. She was ugly in every sense of the word.

She was nothing more than a sad and lonely old lady. Long gone were the days when her male friends called around to see her, and long gone were the all-night parties. No one wanted this decrepit old woman now. All her children had moved away from her. She was a poisonous old hag. She had twelve grandchildren but not one of them visited her.

Mrs Phoenix's world had shrunk. She only ventured out each day to get fags or fresh milk. It took her ages to walk to the corner shop, and she smelled and looked unkempt, so people mostly avoided her. She wore her greasy black hair in a scruffy bun at the top of her head. Her yellowing teeth and phlegmy chest meant no one wanted to get too close, so people would cross the road to avoid her when they saw her approach.

Late one Saturday afternoon, Mrs Phoenix went on her regular walk to the local shop. Her arms ached as she struggled to carry the bags back to her house. The cheap carrier bags strained under the weight of the alcohol. The rain drizzled down on her and she felt cold to her bones. She was relieved when she finally got home. Her body was riddled with arthritis and things that were once so simple were now mammoth tasks. Her body was now as twisted as her mind.

Mrs Phoenix put her bags down on the doorstep and opened her front door. The house was shabby and stank of stale alcohol and a toilet that had not been cleaned in years. It was damp and uninviting. Mrs Phoenix could no longer call on her male friends who used to do odd jobs around the place in exchange for sex, because they were no longer around.

Mrs Phoenix plonked herself in front of the television and sank down into the stained and grubby settee. She placed the eight cans of Strong Brew and packet of Benson and Hedges on the dirty, ash filled coffee table. Just as she was dozing off, she heard a noise in the back yard,

'Those damn kids again,' she thought.

She ignored it but five minutes later she heard it again.

'For God's sake!' She cursed as she dragged her lardy frame to the back door, leaning on the ledge for a breather. She had COPD now and doing anything took a lot of effort.

She opened the back door and as the icy air hit her face, she shivered. It was pitch-black outside. She shouted into the darkness,

'Fuck off and play in your own gardens you little shits.'

She was sick and tired of the local kids knocking on her door or jumping over her back wall. They plagued her. She did not help herself though, the kids loved the way that she reacted to them. She always became enraged, so they did it even more. Just as she was about to close the door, BANG, something hit her full force in the face. Something very heavy. Blood spewed out of her broken nose and onto her lips. It oozed into the deep crevices around her mouth. She tried desperately to work out what was happening, but it was all happening too fast. As she put her hand up to her nose another blow rained down on her from above. CRACK. Her skull split open like an egg and she blacked out. Brain fluid spattered the windowpane.

They say that your hearing is the last sense to go. As Mrs Phoenix hit the ground, she clearly heard the words, ‘Die, you bitch. Die!’ being hissed into the cold night air.

Six days later, one of the local kids jumped over Mrs Phoenix’s garden wall to get his football back. The scene that met him was a blood bath. Mrs Phoenix lay on the floor, frozen and surrounded in a pool of crimson blood.

SHOCKING NEWS

Kira sat in the hairdressers having her highlights done. Her long blonde hair reached halfway down her back. She did not like going to the hairdressers. She did not enjoy the small talk and thought it was a waste of half a day. Kira grabbed herself a pile of magazines and a newspaper and prepared to relax whilst she waited for the dye to take. She picked up the Evening Post from the coffee table in front of her. She hardly ever read the local newspaper but had felt compelled to do so on this day. As she unfolded the paper she froze. The headline jumped off the page.

Pensioner Peggy Phoenix bludgeoned to death in her own home.

Kira instinctively knew that this was Toby's mother. He had often referred to himself and his siblings as the 'Phoenix Clan' as that is what they had been known as on the Bramwell Estate where he grew up. Kira froze in the chair as she read the article.

OAP attacked in her own home found in a sea of blood.

Kira felt sick and did not know what to do. She wanted to get up and leave the shop but couldn't because her hair was still in foils. She thought about the old lady who had possibly been laying in the snow for days on end.

Old lady found in her garden bludgeoned to death by heavy object lay there for days.

As soon as she had left the hairdressers Kira rang Faye.

'Hi Kira, what's up?'

Faye could hear the anxiety in Kira's voice.

Kira told Faye about the newspaper article.

She stumbled nervously over her words and Faye could sense her discomfort.

'Kira, I know it's an upsetting story, but what exactly are you saying here? What are you worried about? What are you imagining?'

Kira felt too panicky to even answer, after a moment of silence Faye spoke.

'Kira, please do not be offended but I think your imagination is running wild with you. There is nothing at all connecting Toby to the murder. He also has six other siblings who would have a possible motive to kill the woman.'

Kira felt so relieved. Faye thought everything was OK.

Faye added, 'Toby's right to confidentiality must over-ride any fantasy that you have imagined about him, Kira. You have absolutely no evidence that he is a killer. He was just sounding off in his counselling sessions.'

Kira knew that Faye was right. She absolutely knew deep down that there was no way Toby could have killed his mother, but she still felt uneasy. She was glad that she had spoken to Faye though, and she felt much calmer for it.

THE APOLOGY

Kira sat at the breakfast bar in her kitchen and flipped open her laptop. She had been qualified for five years now and had decided to venture into private practice. She still worked at the hospital, but she now also saw private clients. She glanced at her emails and one stood out. It was from Toby Phoenix. Nervously she opened it.

Hi Kira,
I really hope you are well. Firstly, I want to apologise for storming out of the hospital. I

guess I felt rejected and I let my temper get the better of me. It was that same feeling of rejection and abandonment that I felt all through my childhood, from my parents, my friends, my teachers, and my family. I behaved like a child and I am so sorry.
You are the only person that I have ever really trusted and felt able to open up to. I know it's a big ask but I wonder whether you would consider counselling me again. My mother was murdered last year, and I need some help with my emotions. I am all over the place. I am desperate. Please will you help me? Can I come and see you? I will understand if you feel you need to say no, and I won't hold it against you if you do. I hope that you reply.
Thanks, Toby.

Kira read the email a few times. She knew that she should tell Toby no, but she wanted to see him and to know what was going on in his head now that his mother was gone. Would he be more open with her? Would he be glad that she was dead? Kira's hand hovered over the computer keyboard. She was not sure what to say.

Hello Toby,
I am sorry to hear about your mother's tragic death. I know that your relationship with her

was difficult, but I imagine that her death has thrown up a lot of feelings for you. Unfortunately, I am not able to counsel you as our relationship became too close. I know that you will be disappointed, but I am sure that you will understand,
Kind regards,
Kira Devlin.

Kira's hand hesitated over the send button. She felt so torn, a part of her wanted to see Toby again. She knew that he was not a monster and she did not want to be yet another person to reject him. That could finish him. His self-concept was so fragile. Kira could hear Faye's voice.

'Kira, you know that it is not ethical for you to work with Toby. He has crossed too many boundaries. He may even be infatuated with you. You must think about your own safety in all this too.'

However, there was something in the last line of Toby's email that interested her. He was not being pushy. He was not pushing the boundary, in fact he was allowing her to say no. Kira deleted the email that she had drafted and wrote another one.

Hello Toby,
I am sorry to hear about the death of your

mother. That must have been such a shock for you. I know that your relationship with her was very difficult, but I also know that her death may have thrown up some stuff for you. I am happy to counsel you. You will find me at sixteen Zouch Street. How does one p.m. next Monday sound?
Kind regards,
Kira

Kira did not need to wait for the reply. She knew that Toby would be there and for some reason she felt excited about the meeting.

SOMETHING CRAZY

Kira's private practice was located on a broad avenue, lined with large oak trees. Her room was on the first floor and large canvases of forests and seascapes adorned the walls. There was a modern art sculpture in the corner of the room. The plush Sherlock chairs were both comfortable and practical, and the room felt light and airy. Toby tapped on the door. Kira as always was dressed impeccably in a trouser suit and heels. She wore her beauty effortlessly. She opened the door to let him in. There was a tension between them, an attraction maybe.

Toby was far more confident than when she had first met him. He initiated the conversation,

'Kira, thank you so much for agreeing to see me.' He looked directly into her eyes and smiled.

'That is OK Toby, but before we start, I have to make sure that you know that we have to be careful.'

'I understand.'

'Let me finish. I need you to understand that this relationship can only be professional. I can only help you in a professional capacity. We absolutely cannot be friends on social media or meet outside of these sessions.'

Toby smiled and nodded, 'OK, OK, I get it Kira, message received and understood.' He saluted jokingly.

Kira gestured for Toby to take a seat, and he began to talk immediately, as if he had been storing things up for a long time.

'I just cannot get my head around what happened to my mother. I know it sounds odd, but it is almost like I put it out there to the Universe and then it happened. I do not even believe in that kind of shit, but it was as if someone read my mind. Don't get me wrong, I fantasied enough times that she would die a slow painful death, but this is something else'.

Kira studied every micro expression on his

face. Was he toying with her? Did he not realise that she would naturally suspect him of killing his mother? But he did not flinch. He seemed genuine, but then again, he never showed much emotion, so it was hard to tell.

'How did you find out about your mother's death, Toby?'

Kira felt herself begin to sweat a little at the back of her neck. She took a sip of water to compose herself.

'The police came around to my house and spoke to Layla. They asked for me.'

'Layla?' enquired Kira, with a puzzled look on her face.

'Oh, Layla, she is my girlfriend. She lives with me.'

Kira wondered if this was the truth. He had never mentioned a girlfriend before. How could he have a girlfriend? He could hardly cope with himself, let alone hold down a relationship.

'Go on,' Kira prompted.

'Well, Layla called me to the door and the police insisted on coming inside. I knew something was up by the expressions on their faces. It was the same look that the policeman had when he told my mother that they had found my father. They asked me if I was Toby Phoenix and I nodded. They told me to sit down. Then the older cop told me that a lady matching my mother's description had been found dead in the backyard of my mother's house. They said that they were not sure it was her, but that one of the family would need to identify her. I did not know at that point that she had been murdered though.'

'So, you knew nothing about the murder at this point?' asked Kira.

'No, it was only a few days later that I found out. They sent a female police officer to 'break it to me gently' but all I felt was relief. It was as if a huge weight had been lifted from my shoulders. Is that awful?'

Kira shook her head and comforted Toby with her eyes.

Toby spent the rest of the session telling Kira that he felt numb. He said he felt nothing at all, almost as if nothing had happened.

'Can I tell you something crazy?' asked Toby.

'Go ahead.'

'Well, I sometimes wonder whether I did it. Maybe I got up in the night and went there, like sleep walking or in a trance or something and battered the crazy bitch to death. Maybe my self-conscious took over. Is that even possible? I mean, you hear about people killing their partners in their sleep, don't you? I have always sleepwalked, sleep talked and had night terrors. Crazy right?'

Kira smiled and nodded kindly at him.

'Yes, that's crazy alright.'

Inside though, Kira still felt disturbed with all this talk. Kira did not know what to feel. She had a heavy feeling in her stomach. She agreed to see Toby at the same time the following week. She decided that she would not tell Faye that she was seeing Toby again, after all, she would only get the wrong end of the stick and see the relationship for something that it was not. Kira knew deep down that Toby was not a dangerous man.

MOVING FORWARD

The following week, Toby turned up for his weekly counselling session and Kira waited for him to start the session. She no longer needed to encourage him to talk. Toby seemed somehow calmer than she had ever seen him before, he looked relaxed, his shoulders looked a little lower and his whole demeanour seemed different.

Toby began to talk. 'I've made some pretty big decisions. My mother's death has had a huge impact on me. It has freed me in a way. I have decided that I can either let my awful childhood affect the rest of my life or I can let it go. I can live a happy life. You have taught me that my past does not necessarily need to dictate my future. You have taught me that I have choices. Since coming to see you, I have realised that I have been living a half-life, but now I am ready to take my future into my own hands and for that I thank you.'

'OK,' said Kira, 'so what does this new future look like for you?'

Toby looked directly at Kira, wanting to gage Kira's reaction.

'I've always held a bit of myself back in relationships. I have always expected people to abandon me because they usually do, but it's time for change. It's time to take a leap of faith.'

'OK,' said Kira again, secretly wishing he would just spit out what he was trying to say.

'So, I have decided to propose to Layla.'

The silence hung between them like a sheet. Toby studied Kira's reaction. He wondered whether she thought it was a good idea, but she was not giving much away.

'Well then, what do you think?' he asked.

Kira was aware that she needed to say something soon.

'It seems that my opinion really matters to you Toby. What is that about? Do you not trust your own judgement?' she asked.

Toby smiled. He knew that she would throw it all back at him. Typical therapist response!

'I value your opinion Kira, that is all.'

Kira stayed non-committal. 'I believe that you know what's best for you Toby. I wish you the best of luck with your future and with whatever decisions you make.'

Toby smiled at Kira. 'Thank you' he said, 'there's more too'.

'Go on,' said Kira intrigued.

'Well, I had a shit childhood. I have always vowed never to have children because I would hate to not be a good father, but I have done a lot of soul searching. I have decided to take control of my life. I am a good man and I can be a good father. I have decided that I want to have children, lots of children as soon as Layla is ready to'.

Kira was taken aback. This all seemed very quick and she wondered what Toby's agenda was by telling her all this. She decided that she needed time to process everything that he had said and her true feelings around it.

'Do you mind if we finish a little earlier Toby? I am not feeling too great.'

'Yes, that's fine,' said Toby, 'I'm pretty tired myself.'

Kira sat back and watched Toby put his jacket on and leave the room. She felt very uneasy.

THE RING

The sun shone brightly through the kitchen window and Layla set about doing some chores. She filled the dishwasher and wiped down the surfaces. She put her favourite songs on the Juke box as she always worked better to music. She set about organising the laundry. She emptied the contents of Toby's gym bag onto the kitchen floor to do his dirty washing. Out with the sweaty gym kit tumbled a small silver box. Layla picked it up and shook it gently. She knew that she should not open it, but she simply could not resist. Slowly and nervously she opened the little box and eagerly peered inside. Wedged in the black velvet cushion was a beautiful sparkling diamond ring which took her breath away. It was the one that she had pointed out to Toby when they had last visited Tenby, a quaint little seaside resort that they both loved. Layla knew that Toby was going to propose to her and could not conceal her excitement. She jumped up and down banging her fists frantically in the air. She adored Toby. She knew that he was still troubled by his past, but she loved him and knew that she wanted to spend the rest of her life with him. She believed that she could help Toby to get over his demons.

Layla carefully placed the ring back in its box, flipped the lid down and put it back in Toby's bag. A huge smile spread over her face as she wondered how Toby was going to propose. He was a deep and sensitive man but not one prone to romantic gestures. Layla wondered whether Toby would get down on bended knee or maybe he would propose in a more modern way. She enjoyed thinking about this and found herself smiling for the rest of that day, deliriously happy.

THE NEWCOMER

Layla loved her weekly yoga class, because it helped her to relax and to feel connected, but this week was extra special as she had news. She was going to tell her yoga friends about Toby's imminent proposal. She had become close to the 'yoga girls' over the last few months. Her stomach lurched with excitement as she entered the Serenity Suite at her local gym. Rosie, the instructor stood in the corner of the room organising her equipment and preparing for the class.

Layla greeted her friends. As they chatted, she

spotted a new face. The newcomer had a short structured red bob and was strikingly attractive. Layla thought to herself, 'She doesn't look like a yoga type. She is far too manicured and structured. Yoga lovers have loose natural hair.' Layla then smiled to herself as she realised how judgmental and stereotypical she was being, but all the same, Layla was annoyed that there was a newcomer in the group.

Rosie addressed the group,

'Hello everyone. As you can see, we have a newcomer here today so let's all make Cerys feel welcome.'

The ladies waved at the newcomer and prepared themselves for their class.

'Before we start, do you have any health conditions that I should know about?' Rosie asked Cerys

'No, I don't have any health issues, although I am pregnant.'

'Well, that's not a problem. None of the positions are dangerous for pregnant women. Just take it easy as it is your first time doing yoga,' said Rosie kindly.

The women chatted amongst themselves whilst Rosie dimmed the lights and put on some relaxing music. They all rolled out their mats and filled up their water bottles. Layla decided that today was not a good day to tell her yoga friends about Toby's imminent proposal. She did not want to share personal news when there was a stranger in the group. She was disappointed but knew it could wait for a few weeks. Rosie guided the class through various breathing and relaxation exercises and then she started on the different yoga positions. Layla caught sight of herself in the mirror and smiled to herself. She imagined what Toby would think if he could see her doing the 'cat cow' and the 'downward dog.' He always teased her about her yoga poses.

As the class came to an end, Layla decided to let go of her annoyance at the newcomer's presence, and instead decided to get to know her better. Layla rolled up her mat and crossed the room to chat to Cerys. Cerys was funny and interesting and before they knew it, they had been chatting in the doorway for half an hour. Layla suggested they go for a coffee so they could chat properly, and Cerys agreed.

The two women looked like they had been friends for years as they made their way to the coffee shop. Cerys ordered a caramel latte and Layla ordered her usual green tea. Then they headed to the comfy chocolate sofas in the corner of the room and the conversation flowed easily between the pair. Cerys was easy going and Layla felt like she had known her forever. Before long, the pair were laughing comfortably together. To the outsider they looked like age-old friends.

'So, when are you due?' asked Layla pointing to Cerys' pregnant stomach.

'30th of March,' said Cerys.

'Would you like to see some photos?'

Layla looked confused.

Cerys smiled, 'We had a 4D scan done and got lots of photos.'

'Oh right,' said Layla as the penny dropped. 'Yes, of course, I'd love to see some photos.'

Cerys handed Layla her sequin encrusted iPhone.

'Scroll to the right.'

Layla took the phone and started scrolling through the photos.

'Oh Wow! You can see the baby's face clearly. Look at his little hands! You can even see the fingers! How amazing is that?!' exclaimed Layla.

Whilst she looked through the photos, Layla wondered whether she and Toby would have children one day, but then she drew her attention back to Cerys. She slowly scrolled through the photos, taking in every detail, and smiling. Then her heart missed a beat. There was a photo of Toby, her Toby, smiling back at her.

'What's wrong?' asked Cerys, sensing Layla's discomfort.

'Why have you got a photo of my boyfriend on your phone?' asked Layla, pointing at the photo of Toby.

'There must be some mistake,' said Cerys. 'This is my partner Toby, he's the father of my baby'.

Layla's world swirled. Emotions and thoughts bombarded her. She could not process what she was hearing. She grabbed her bag and rushed to the door without even saying goodbye to Cerys. Cerys chased after her saying that there must be have been a mistake, but Layla had already run to her car.

Layla drove home on autopilot. She pulled up at her house and the full realisation of what had happened hit her. Layla let herself into the house and then fell to the floor. She pulled her knees up to her chest and sobbed uncontrollably. She remained on the floor for hours. It was only when she got too cold that she finally got to her feet. Then the anger kicked in.

'How dare he do this to me! I have supported him through so much,' Layla thought.

Suddenly everything made sense to her, like the amounts of time spent 'exercising' or 'at the gym', the fact that Toby had been so distant, and the ring. The ring! It was probably for Cerys. Layla was furious, so furious that she could not think properly. She chose to say nothing to Toby until she had decided what she wanted to do.

THE DENIAL

Layla was sitting on the settee when she heard Toby's car pull up onto the driveway. The familiar sound of his key turning in the lock usually filled her with excitement, but today it filled her with sheer dread. Toby popped his head around the lounge door and said hi to Layla. Then he went into the kitchen and poured himself a pint of cold water. Layla followed him into the kitchen. Toby knocked the water back in one go as if it was a refreshing lager, then turned his attention to Layla.

'Hey, honey, how are you? How's your day

been?'

Layla looked at him. He seemed so normal, yet she knew he was leading a double life.

How could he behave so normal? she thought.

'I'm fine,' she said but her voice quavered and gave her away immediately. She had not planned to let on straight away that she knew about Toby's other woman, but her voice had betrayed her.

'Hey Honey, what's the matter?' said Toby frowning with concern.

Layla still could not believe that Toby was acting so normal. If she did not know better, she would think he really cared for her. He certainly was good at switching his concern on. He looked genuinely concerned about her. Layla took a deep breath in then looked Toby in the eye.

'You want to know what's the matter? You want to know what the hell's the matter?' she screamed.

Toby did a double take. He could not believe the state that Layla was in. He did not know what to say. He was in total shock.

'Look, I don't know what I'm meant to have done and I can't defend myself if you're not going to enlighten me,' said Toby.

'I'll enlighten you alright,' Layla spat. 'I know about Cerys and I know about the baby and everything. Do not even bother trying to deny it!

I've seen the photos of you on her phone and the baby scans.'

Toby recoiled. He did not know what to say or do, he was frozen to the spot. Finally, he spoke,

'Layla, I genuinely don't know what the hell you are talking about. I can see that you are upset but I honestly do not know anyone called Cerys and I have no idea about any baby either.'

That was the catalyst that tipped Layla over the edge. She could not believe that Toby was denying even knowing Cerys. She thought that she meant more to him than that. She had hoped he was going to tell her he had made a mistake, that he had had a fling but that it was her that he really wanted. She had hoped that he would have had an explanation for this other woman; maybe that she was deranged or black mailing him. But no! He was just going to deny even knowing her!

Layla ran up the stairs into the bedroom and pulled all Toby's clothes off the hangers. She piled them into black bags and started throwing them down the stairs. Toby tried to talk to her, but it was no use now. She was incapable of listening because she was too angry and screaming so much.

Toby decided to leave the house to give Layla time to calm down. He hoped he could talk properly to her when he returned and solve this misunderstanding.

'I'm going to give you some space. I'll be back in a few hours and we can talk. Please, Layla, be reasonable.' Toby pleaded. He grabbed his jacket, car keys, and mobile and headed outside.

Layla was like a woman on a mission. She took everything of Toby's out of the wardrobe and chucked them into bin bags and threw them all onto the driveway. She picked up the numerous photos that adorned their house and flung them against the brick walls. Glass scattered everywhere like confetti. She really wanted to hurt Toby. She smashed up all his precious vinyl records, gashing her hands and getting covered in blood in the process. Then she began to cry, and the sobs overtook her. She had no control over them, and they came in almighty waves. She slid her back against the wall and fell to the floor in a crouching position, and she stayed like that for ages.

Later that evening, Toby phoned Layla's mobile. He rang and rang but Layla ignored it. After two hours, there was a knock at the door. Layla knew it was Toby. He did not use his key for fear of further upsetting Layla. Layla put the chain on the door and bolted the inner locks. She did not want to see him or speak to him.

'Go away, Toby. I have nothing to say to you!'

'Layla, please. I need to speak to you. I need to put things right,' begged Toby.

Layla ignored Toby and went into the lounge and turned the music up loud to drown out Toby's frantic pleas. Toby knew that it was pointless trying to talk to Layla tonight. He decided he would return in the morning and try again. He angrily kicked at the black bags on the drive and made his way back to his car. He decided to sleep somewhere in his car and return in the morning. He was so confused.

TOBY'S ARREST

Toby did not manage to get any sleep in the car. He was cold, hungry, and upset and desperate to sort things out with Layla. He picked up his mobile and tried to ring her, but she was clearly ignoring his calls. He tried at least twenty times to contact her, but it was useless, so he decided to go home and see her.

Toby pulled up on the driveway and walked up the gravel path. He rang the doorbell but there was no answer. He banged on the door with his fist.

'Layla, please, come on, just open the door and

let me talk to you.'

He was met with stony silence. He walked around the back of the house and peered through the French doors, but Layla was nowhere to be seen. He knocked on the windows and shouted again but to no avail. He was so confused. He knew that Layla had the wrong end of the stick but until she agreed to talk to him, he could do nothing about it. He grew increasingly frustrated. Over and over in his mind, Toby replayed what Layla had said about Cerys and the baby. None of it made any sense. He wondered whether someone had a personal vendetta against Layla, but he could think of no-one who would. She was such a sweet girl and she never fell out with anyone. His head hurt thinking about it all.

After waiting at the house for over an hour Toby finally gave up and left. Over the next few weeks, Toby tried over and over to get in touch with Layla. He sent numerous text messages, left voicemails, and called to the house but Layla refused to answer. He sent flowers and left notes on her car windscreen, but his actions were met with total silence.

Toby had no choice but to continue sleeping in his car. He had no one else to turn to. He no longer kept in touch with any of his siblings. They all carried a certain amount of shame and found it easier not to see each other. Toby had very few friends as he found it hard to form attachments with people. Toby got hardly any sleep in the car. Even though he was a strapping guy he felt vulnerable in the car. It was also bitterly cold.

On the fifth day, Toby awoke to someone banging their fist on his car window. He squinted his eyes. The early morning sun was just rising but Toby had not long dropped off to sleep. He wound down his window and peered up at the police officer who was looking at him.

'Are you Toby Phoenix?' the officer asked.

Toby uttered 'What?' in a state of confusion. He could not work out what he had done wrong.

'You heard me alright! Are you Toby Phoenix or what?' asked the officer again more forcefully and with growing impatience.

'Yes, yes I am. What's wrong? Is it Layla? Oh God, is she OK? Please tell me she's OK?' said Toby. He felt panic rise through his body.

'Step out of the car sir,' demanded the officer.

Toby realised that the quicker he got out of the car, the quicker that the officer would tell him what had happened to Layla.

I hope she hasn't done anything stupid he thought.

'Put your hands above your head where I can see them,' snarled the officer.

Now Toby was really confused and desperate

to know what was going on.

'Phoenix, I am arresting you for harassment. You do not have to say anything, but it may harm your defence if you do not mention when questioned something which you later rely on in court, anything you do say may be given in evidence.'

Toby's mind swirled fervently like autumn leaves in the wind. He truly could not make sense of anything that was being said to him. The officer handcuffed him and ordered him to get in the back of the patrol car. Toby did so, he lacked the energy to resist. Toby sat silently in the back of the patrol car, his gaze fixed firmly into the mid distance, unaware of what was going on around him. He had shut down.

After about twenty minutes, they reached the station. Toby looked up, realising that they had stopped. The officer ordered him out of the car and took him into the police station. Toby was checked in by the custody sergeant and then shown to a small room. He sat down and waited to find out what this was all about.

'Do you know Layla Johnson?' asked the officer.

'Yes of course I do, I live with her. She's my girlfriend, or at least I did live with her until…' said Toby.

'Enough of the small talk,' the officer cut in,

'just answer the damn questions son! Have you been bombarding Layla with phone calls and texts?'

Toby stared silently in disbelief. He could not believe what was happening. The questions kept coming at him.

'Have you been stalking the property? Have you turned up at her place of work? Have you been making a nuisance of yourself?' asked the officer.

Every time Toby tried to explain the situation, the police officer shut him up. Eventually Toby gave up and stopped trying to explain, instead he just sat there angry and upset. The officer gave him a formal warning and told him that they would be watching him closely. After eight hours in custody, Toby was finally released and given strict instructions to stay away from Layla.

Toby felt like he was going mad or that the world was going mad. Just as things were starting to look up, this happened! He felt helpless and did not know how to fix the situation. He desperately wanted to see Layla and to put things right, but that would mean breaking his bail conditions and being sent to prison for harassment and stalking. He knew that he needed to speak to Kira. She always managed to help him to make sense of his tangled thoughts and feelings. She had the knack of helping him to calm down. He rang her and asked if she could see him later that day, ahead of their scheduled appointment on Wednesday. Thankfully, Kira agreed.

DESPERATION

Toby ran all the way to Kira's practice and entered the counselling room without even knocking. Kira could see immediately that Toby was in a bad way. His face was taught and grey and he began talking before he had even sat down.

'Things are really screwed up Kira. Someone is messing with my head. This woman has told Layla that I am the father of her unborn baby and she believes her. She won't talk to me, so I can't even tell her it's not true. To top it all off, Layla has gone to the police and said I am harassing her, and I’ve been arrested and warned to stay away from her and have absolutely no contact with her whatsoever!’

Kira took a deep breath because she was not quite sure where to begin. She managed to calm Toby down and got him to tell her the story properly.

‘Toby, are you going to do what the police have said?’

Kira needed to know that he was not going to try to contact Layla. This was important. Toby just looked at her. He did not answer.

SIX MONTHS LATER

Layla had been miserable without Toby. She had lost weight and could not sleep properly. Deep down she did not believe that he was capable of such deceit. She had cried herself to sleep for weeks; she had screamed and ranted. Her friends had all urged her to move on with her life, but that was easier said than done. One friend had even said that she had never liked Toby anyway. She thought he was weird. Something told Layla that Toby was innocent, even though the evidence against him was overwhelming.

Over the last few months, she had started to

think about the whole situation logically. She had started to doubt Cerys's authenticity. Who was this woman? She had come from nowhere and did not even seem suited to yoga. In addition, no one had seen Cerys at yoga since that day. Layla had asked Rosie to give her Cerys' phone number or address so that she could speak to her about her relationship with Toby. Rosie reluctantly breached data protection and did so, knowing how much it meant to Layla, but when Layla had rung the phone number it was dead. Layla had tried to find Cerys on Facebook, but she was not on there.

Layla had also been thinking a lot about the photos on Cerys' phone. Something had seemed oddly familiar about the photo of Cerys and Toby on the seafront. Maybe Cerys had superimposed herself onto Toby's photo? Layla pulled out her phone and clicked on Toby's Facebook profile. She had unfriended him months ago, but his account was public, so she could still see his posts. She clicked on 'photos' then 'profile photos, she scrolled through them. Suddenly she froze. There it was! There was a picture of Toby sitting on an old stone wall near the seafront. He was on his own. Cerys must have digitally superimposed herself sitting next to him. You could do anything with green screen technology these days. As for the baby scan pictures, there are plenty of them on the internet. Layla had not checked the name on the scans. Why would she have? Layla had gradually concluded that Cerys was an imposter. For whatever reason, she had wanted to hurt Layla and she had succeeded. Also, if Toby were seeing this woman, he would be with her now and he wasn't. She had heard from friends that he was living in a flat in Uplands and she often drove past. She could see Toby in the flat from the road, always alone.

Layla felt awful when she knew that she had been too rash with Toby. She needed to find out the truth. She needed to see him. She picked up her mobile and clicked on his number.

MAKING UP

Toby had managed to find himself a small flat. It was only a one bedroom with a tiny lounge but it sure beat sleeping in the car. He slumped on the couch and flicked on the television. Suddenly his mobile rang, and Layla's name flashed across the screen, he picked up immediately.

'Layla, is that you?'

For a moment, the line was silent, and Toby's heart sank but then Layla spoke,

'Hi Toby, how are you?'

'I'm OK but I miss you. I love you Layla and

I want to be with you. I don't understand any of this, but I am willing to do whatever it takes to win you back. Please honey just give me a chance.'

'Can you meet me somewhere Toby? I will totally understand if you say no, but there are things I need to talk to you about. I need to get things straight in my head. I have been doing a lot of thinking and some things don't add up.'

Without hesitation Toby agreed to meet her. He was amazed that Layla wanted to see him but also very confused. He wondered what she wanted after all this time. They agreed to meet at Vesuvius, a lovely little Italian restaurant perched high on the clifftops, in a little village called Mumbles. Toby offered to pick Layla up, but she insisted on meeting him there.

GOOD NEWS

Toby tapped on Kira's door and entered the therapy room. Kira could see that he had news, she wondered what it was but avoided asking him.

'Layla has been in touch with me! She wants us to meet up to discuss things. I am so happy!'

Kira felt uncomfortable. He should not be seeing her, it wasn't right.

'What did you say?' Kira asked nervously.

'We are meeting at Vesuvius on Friday night. With a bit of luck, she will have calmed down and we can finally sort this mess out.'

Kira knew that it was not her place as Toby's counsellor to give him advice, but she strongly believed that Toby's relationship with Layla was detrimental. She knew that her next question was leading.

'Do you think that it's a good idea to meet her Toby? What about the police conditions… you know, the harassment order?'

'Oh, that expired after six months anyway,' said Toby.

Kira wondered if there was anything that she could say to stop Toby seeing Layla but could think of nothing. She felt irritated. She wanted to tell Toby to leave Layla alone, but she knew that it wasn't her place to do so. Instead she said,

'OK, you know what's best for you. I hope it all goes well for you'.

REUNION DATE

Toby took ages to get ready for his meeting with Layla. He ironed his favourite shirt and splashed on expensive aftershave. He was nervous but eager to finally see her. He arrived at the restaurant half an hour early; he knew how much it used to annoy Layla when he was late. He ordered some red wine and sat looking out of the window. The sea was rough but still beautiful, it's dark grey waves majestically danced on the shoreline. He kept looking nervously at the door, eagerly anticipating Layla's arrival.

Layla had also made a special effort. She had

had her hair done and wore the red dress that Toby loved. She turned the music up loud on her car radio. There was something exhilarating about driving on a clifftop with the music at full blast. Layla had butterflies in her stomach. She could not wait to see Toby. They had agreed to meet at Vesuvius at 7.30 p.m.

The road which led to the restaurant in Mumbles was carved through the rocks. It was a narrow winding road with wonderful views over the bay below.

Layla smiled as she sang along with the music. The sun was just setting and the last of the sunlight was just disappearing. Layla drove slightly faster than she should have but she was eager to get to the restaurant. Her car weaved around the clifftop road and she admired the sea below her. As Layla took the bend, a car came hurtling towards her on her side of the road forcing her to veer to the left. She slammed on the brakes and skidded for at least ten seconds, but it was too late. She was too close to the edge. Her car was veering over the cliff top. There was a sheer drop of about eighty feet into the choppy sea. Layla screamed as her car left the road. Her car bounced against the craggy rocks as it plummeted down towards the sea. Layla was thrown violently from side to side. Her head hit the driver's window with force and blood poured down her face. Her neck twisted and contorted as she fell through the air. Her life flashed before her. Toby's face flashed before her.

Everything seemed to happen in slow motion. Layla knew that she was in trouble. She prayed that she would survive. She screamed for help. The sea was fast approaching. The car sliced through it like a knife. It was a high tide and the car sank ten metres down. Layla was semi-conscious at this point, but badly concussed from the fall. She struggled to undo the seat belt, but she was confused, and her hands did not seem to work.

The people on the Pier who had witnessed the car plunge into the sea began to move. They started shouting and screaming. An old guy fumbled with his mobile phone and dialled 999.

'999 What's your emergency sir?'

'Um, ah, err… an ambulance… and a fire engine, I think. I don't know! The lifeboat! A car has gone over the cliff edge into the sea. There was a lady inside. Come quickly!'

One lady threw off her coat and dived into the sea, trying to help Layla. She swam down to the car, but the water was cold, and she simply could not stand the pressure that deep. She swam back to the surface, gulped in a deep breath and attempted to get to Layla one last time. On lookers shouted at her to come out of the water worried that she too would drown.

The police turned up first and seconds later an ambulance and the lifeboat arrived. The police dived into the water to try to help but they could not see anything. They radioed for diving masks and gas cylinders and the area was quickly cordoned off whilst statements were taken from those that had witnessed the accident. Gradually, more of a crowd built as people stopped to see what had happened.

Toby waited patiently at the restaurant for two hours. He repeatedly phoned Layla, but her phone went straight to answer machine. Toby knew that Layla would have a good reason for being late. After two hours, he knew that she was not coming so with a heavy heart he paid the drinks bill and left. He was feeling worried now. It crossed his mind that this was Layla's way of getting revenge.

As he headed home on the winding cliff top road, he got caught up in the backlog of traffic caused by the accident. The traffic jam trailed for miles on end. People got out of their cars to try and find out what the delay was. Toby wondered what on earth had happened in this sleepy little seaside town, so he got out of his car and asked a group of people what had happened. One lady was keen to tell him everything.

'I saw it all happen. A red convertible Beetle was driving too fast and on the wrong side of the road and forced an oncoming car to go over the edge. The car came clean off the road. It flew through the air like a missile and then plunged into the sea.'

'What was the car?' asked Toby, but he knew the answer before the lady even said anything.

'It was a Silver Volkswagen Polo,' said the woman.

Toby looked down at the water. Two divers came trudging slowly out of the sea. One of them held a limp body in his arms. It was almost dark, but Toby instinctively knew that it was Layla. A gut-wrenching wail emerged from somewhere deep inside him and he dropped to his knees. His arms rose to his head shielding his face and his hands involuntarily clenched into fists. Then everything went completely black.

THE HOSPITAL

The paramedics at the crash scene had taken Toby to Mount Heath Hospital. They had heavily sedated him on the way as he had become combative. He had been in a deep sleep for over twenty-four hours when gradually he started to stir. He began to move his limbs and struggled to open his eyes, but they felt as if they had been glued down. He felt groggy and disorientated, his legs felt like lead and he tried to move his arm but there was something attached to it holding it down. A nurse spotted him moving and rushed to his bedside to soothe him.

'It's OK Toby, relax, you are at Mount Heath Hospital. You have had a terrible shock and we had to sedate you.'

Toby squinted and frowned at the nurse. He could hardly see her or work out what she was saying…… A shock… Sedate you….

The nurse repeated her words and gently touched his shoulder. Toby could not take in what she was telling him.

Suddenly it all came flooding back. Vesuvius! The divers! Layla! The image of Layla's lifeless body being carried out of the water kept flashing in his mind. He could not get this image out of his head. He felt as if he was back at the scene. He closed his eyes and started to cry. He sobbed and his whole body convulsed. The nurse stayed with him. She tried to give him a little more sedation, but he angrily pushed her away.

'Is there someone we can call for you Toby? You have had a terrible shock. You blacked out. This can happen sometimes with shock. It is a nervous system reaction. It is the body's way of protecting the mind. Has it happened to you before?'

Toby remained silent. Toby did not want the nurse to call anyone, but the nurse told him it was unsafe to let him out of the hospital in his condition without someone to support him. Other than Layla, Toby had virtually no one. He contemplated ringing his brother Nathan, but quickly decided that he would rather stay in hospital then stoop that low. There was only one person he could think of. He picked up his phone and dialled Kira's number.

'Kira, I need your help. Please help me.' begged Toby.

'Toby, what's wrong? I've been trying to contact you,' said Kira.

Toby had not turned up for his scheduled counselling appointment that morning.

'I'm at the hospital. Something terrible has happened. I have had one of my episodes. I blacked out and they had to sedate me. The hospital will not let me out if they think I have no support. I know that I am really pushing my luck, but will you come to the hospital and say that you will keep an eye on me? You do not actually have to stay with me, just tell a little lie to get me out of here. I'm perfectly safe, I'm not going to top myself, but the hospital want reassurance. Please Kira, I need you,' said Toby.

Kira knew that it was now her who was blurring boundaries, but she could not bear the thought of Toby being stuck at the hospital. She no longer had to worry about Faye admonishing her so she decided that she would break the rules and get Toby out of the hospital.

Kira turned up at the hospital first thing the

next morning. She politely introduced herself to Toby's consultant, explaining that she was a friend of his. The consultant gave Kira an overview of what had happened and told Kira to keep a close eye on Toby. Kira signed some paperwork to say that she would be checking in with Toby regularly. She did not use her real name because she knew she could get into trouble for continuing to counsel Toby and having a connection with him. She did not want to risk losing her job. Once the paperwork was signed, the hospital discharged Toby.

Kira made her way to Toby's bed. He looked washed out, black circles hung under his eyes and he was deathly pale. Toby told Kira what had happened. He was devastated and Kira held him as he sobbed.

After collecting Toby's medication, they left the ward and drove away from the hospital in silence. Both were deep in thought. Kira was thinking about the trouble that she could get into for what she had done. Toby was thinking about the accident. He was aware that he had forgotten something important, but with all the drugs in his system he struggled to remember what it was. It was something about the accident, but he could not put his finger on it.

THE PENNY DROPS

Toby had only been home from hospital for two days when there was a frantic knock on the door. He opened the door to be confronted by two burly police officers.

'Are you Toby Phoenix? We need you to come down to the police station to answer some questions please.'

Toby was confused. The Valium that he had taken just made things worse.

'Why? What's wrong?" asked Toby.

'We just want to ask you some questions about Layla Johnson sir.'

Toby did not have the emotional energy to protest. He grabbed his hoodie and his house keys and followed the officers into their patrol car. When they arrived at the station, they took Toby into an interview room and set up the recording system. Toby was so confused. The older police officer explained to Toby that there were some 'issues' surrounding Layla's death. Numerous eyewitnesses had said that her car had been virtually forced off the road by an oncoming vehicle. Witnesses had reported that it had looked intentional, as if someone has wanted Layla to crash! Toby could not take this in. Someone intentionally wanted to harm Layla. That meant she had been murdered! It was not an accident. Toby felt like the ground was no longer beneath his feet. His brain whirred. He could not keep up, and yet he was still trying to process something about the accident. It was just out of reach.

'Look Toby, we know that you harassed Layla Johnson, and that you bombarded her with phone calls and texts. We know that your relationship ended suddenly and then you stalked her. We also know from Layla's phone records that she had arranged to meet you on the night that she died. As far as we are aware, she had told no one of her plans for that evening. We know that she was angry with you for fathering a baby with some other girl. We know life would be easier for you if Layla disappeared. Tell us about your movements on the night that Layla died Toby.'

'You have got this all wrong! I went to Vesuvius at about seven p.m. to meet Layla. She was the one who rang me to arrange the meeting. Here, you can check my phone records. I swear that I am telling the truth. I admit that I plagued Layla a bit after the breakup, but only because I loved her so much. I wanted her back. I wanted her to understand that she had got things all wrong. I even took a diamond ring to the restaurant with me because if things went well, I was going to propose to her. Ask the restaurant manager. I had asked him to turn the lights down and bring over some roses if I asked for a bottle of champagne… that was my code.'

Toby looked up at the police officers and could see that they did not believe a word he had said.

'That would make a great alibi Mr Phoenix,' said the older officer.

Toby could not comprehend what he was hearing. He could not believe that they thought he would harm Layla. If he had not been so scared, he would have felt enraged. He knew that if they decided to try and pin this on him there was nothing he could do. He had a criminal record longer than his arm. He knew that on paper he looked like a wrong'un and they would soon jump to conclusions. Toby's right leg began to shake up and down uncontrollably under the table. He started to get distressed. The officers suggested that he speak to a lawyer and told him they were keeping him in overnight

Toby was ordered to strip, and the officers gave him some prison clothes. He was led to a cell at the far end of the station. There was a bed, a table, and a small window. Toby lay down on the hard bed and tried to think but it was like thinking through treacle. He simply could not hang on to the thoughts that entered his head. There was one thought that kept creeping into his awareness then slipping quickly back out again. The more Toby tried to grab it, the more it hid away. Eventually Toby fell asleep with Layla's smiling face in his mind.

At three a.m. Toby sat bolt upright in bed, beads of sweat on his furrowed brow. The image slammed him in the face. A red Beetle convertible! The lady at the scene of the accident said a red Beetle convertible drove Layla off the road. Kira drove a red convertible! He knew this because he had seen her get in it when he had bumped into her at the cemetery. Toby wondered whether he was jumping to conclusions, but he could not shift this feeling in his gut. Kira had taught him to listen to his gut.

'It's usually very intuitive,' she had said.

Toby started to piece it all together. There was

only one person that knew Layla would be at the restaurant that night, Kira. She had seemed overly interested in his relationship with Layla. Initially he had not thought too much about Kira turning up at his local park whilst he walked his dog, but he remembered telling her that he walked in Golden Grove Park daily. She always acted so strangely when he saw her there. He had also thought it a bit strange when Kira had turned up at the cemetery when he went to his mate's funeral, but he had put it down to coincidence. It suddenly dawned on him: Kira had been stalking him!

At 9 a.m. the next morning, Toby's solicitor arrived. He had a chat with Toby about the accusations and Toby told him that he was innocent. Toby was now preoccupied with speaking to Kira. He had to find out if his theory was right. After his solicitor left, an officer came in and told Toby that he was being released without charge. They had nothing on him other than their suspicions. Toby knew it would only be a matter of time before they called him back in and pinned Layla's death on him. He knew he had to act quickly and find Layla's killer himself.

As soon as Toby got outside, he typed the name 'Kira Devlin' into Google. Her name came up on the electoral roll and he found her address. Toby ran the three miles from the police station to Kira's house without stopping. He arrived out of breath and pumped with adrenalin. He banged on the door repeatedly with his fist, unsure of exactly what he was going to say when she answered but sure that she was deranged.

Kira opened the door and looked surprised but pleased to see Toby.

'Oh, Toby. Why are you here? You should not be here,' said Kira coyly.

Toby pushed his way past her into the house.

'Kira, where were you on Friday night? Where is your car?'

Toby was still thinking that maybe he had got it wrong. After all, thousands of people have red convertible Beetles. He could be wrong.

Kira said nothing but smiled at Toby.

'Look, I know that you have been stalking me. You turned up at my local park and I tried to ignore it. You even turned up at the cemetery when I had told you I was going to Duffy's funeral. You turn up at all the places where you know I will be. You bombard me with text messages. You are the only other person that knew that Layla was going to Vesuvius on Friday night. So, answer me Kira. Where were you on Friday night? Did you crash into Layla?'

Kira just smiled seductively at him and this infuriated Toby. He grabbed her around the throat with one hand and pushed her hard against the wall.

'You fucking bitch! I trusted you. I let you into my head and you do this!'

Kira gasped for breath, the colour draining from her cheeks. Toby released his grip.

'Everything that I have done, I did for you Toby.'

'What do you mean everything you have done?'

Toby glared at her, totally confused.

'I sorted things out for you Toby. I sorted things out for us to be together.'

In this moment, the full horror of what she meant dawned on him. He realised she was a complete fantasist! Deluded! A psychopath!

'Toby, I know that you are in love with me. I feel the same way about you. I have just cleared the way for us to be happy, to be together. You are finally free. They did not deserve you Toby and now they are gone.'

Toby froze. 'They? Who are you talking about Kira? Who are 'they'?'

'Toby, your mother did not deserve to live, she was an evil old bitch and Layla was just an obstacle in our way.'

Toby was reeling. He could not believe what Kira was saying.

'But why? Why Kira?'

'I knew it was what you wanted darling. I

know you better than you know yourself. I knew that you wanted that old hag dead and I knew that you wanted Layla gone so that we could be together. You did not actually say that, but I just knew Toby, because I know you so well.'

It all finally clicked into place. Kira was so obsessed with him that she had killed his mother and murdered his girlfriend. Toby lost all control at this point and lunged toward Kira. She turned quickly and picked up a knife from the knife block. Toby continued to move towards her and tried to get the knife out of her hand. They grappled with the knife, but Kira kneed him in the groin and managed to get the knife. She plunged the knife deep into his abdomen. Then she twisted it hard.

'You are an ungrateful bastard Toby. If I cannot have you, no one will. I have done so much for you!'

Toby fell to the floor and thoughts flooded his brain. Things had never been clearer. Kira was pure evil. Blood seeped through Toby's clothing and he soon lost consciousness as blood pooled around his body and his eyes grew distant. Kira picked up her phone and dialled 999.

'Help me!! Please come quickly! I have stabbed a man. I think he is dead. He is on my kitchen floor. There's a lot of blood. Please come quickly.'

Kira put the phone down and made herself a nice cup of tea.

THE FINAL ACT

Within ten minutes of Kira's frantic 999 call, the police and an ambulance crew were at her door. The paramedics tried to resuscitate Toby. They put paddles on his chest and shocked him. His limbs flailed in the air, but he remained lifeless. They tried this numerous times. A female officer sat with Kira who was now staring into space. At 3.33 p.m. Toby was declared dead and a blanket was draped over his lifeless body. Kira watched as he was put into the back of the ambulance. Sally, a female police officer, escorted Kira to the Central Police

Station.

Kira was asked to put her clothes and shoes into a plastic bag for evidence and samples were taken from under her nails. Sally took photos of the angry red marks around Kira's throat. Then she took a statement from her. Sally was extremely calm and reassuring.

'Kira, I know this is difficult, but I need you to tell me what happened this afternoon. Take your time, just say what happened in your own words.'

During her time as a counsellor, Kira had seen hundreds of patients telling their trauma stories. She knew exactly how to behave. She rocked slightly and wrung her hands as she spoke, making sure to avoid Sally's eye contact. Every now and then she stopped talking when things got too much.

'Toby Phoenix was an ex patient of mine. I am a counsellor. I saw him at Mount Heath Hospital for a few years, but I had to terminate the sessions as he became too close to me. He had been sexually, physically and emotionally abused by his mother and her lovers. He was what we in the trade call a psychopath, incapable of feeling real emotions. He told me that he had been having black outs where he was unaware of his behaviour. He was stalking me. He followed me to the park where I go running, turned up at the cemetery when I visited my parents' grave, followed me to supervision. He even sent me flowers on Valentine's day. My supervisor, Faye, warned me that he was becoming infatuated with me. She told me to terminate our counselling relationship, which I did. I knew he was a dangerous man but had no idea he was so violent. He told me time and time again that he fantasised about killing his mother, but I didn't think he would actually do it. He could not cope with losing Layla, his girlfriend. If you check your records, then you will see that he has a history of harassment and stalking. Layla had to have a restraining order put on him.'

'So, what happened today Kira?' asked Sally.

'He turned up at my house, all sweaty and agitated. He barged his way in. I could see that he was fired up, so I tried to calm him down. I asked him to leave but he started telling me how much he loved me. He said that he had killed Layla so that we could be together. He also said he had killed 'the bitch', meaning his mother. I was petrified. He tried to kiss me, but I pushed him off, so he grabbed me around the throat. I thought he was going to strangle me. I managed to grab a knife from the counter, but he was grabbing at my wrist. I was screaming for help. He pushed the blade toward my chest. He was going to kill me. He said he would rather me be dead than with anyone other than him. I managed to knee him between the legs and grab the knife off him. I plunged it into his stomach, and he dropped to the floor. It was awful. I was so scared that he was going to kill me like he had killed the others.' Kira stopped talking and sobbed uncontrollably.

'OK Kira, thank you. Let's take a break now.'

Sally brought Kira a coffee and told her to get some sleep. Kira thought that she had performed amazingly.

PATIENT 662908

After five long hours of intensive police interviews, Kira was finally released. Sally explained that the Crown Prosecution Service would decide whether Kira would be prosecuted for Toby's death.

Kira went home that day and logged onto Toby's Facebook account. She had hacked it months ago and had changed some of his statuses and downloaded all of his photos. She knew that if he thought he was going insane then he would see her more often. She erased the account and then made herself a coffee. She felt nothing.

Kira went out into the garden and lit the fire pit. She felt sad for herself. She had begun to believe her own lies about Toby. She had lost the man who truly loved her. She ran her fingers through the red bob wig and then put it on the fire. Time to say goodbye now to Cerys. She also burnt the receipt from the florist from when she had sent herself flowers to cheer herself up on Valentines.

In her hand, she held a file of counselling notes written about her. She read them one last time before also putting them on the fire:

Patient 662908 was abused physically and emotionally from birth by her mother and stepfather. She was diagnosed with reactive attachment disorder aged eight and struggled to make meaningful relationships with anyone. Aged ten, she caused a car crash in which both her parents died. She claimed to have no memory of the crash and said she had some sort of absence. She lived in foster homes until she reached eighteen. There the abuse continued. She severely injured two of her foster siblings and was eventually put in a secure unit. She was diagnosed with Borderline Personality Disorder aged twenty along with Psychopathy. She is extremely charming, highly intelligent yet very manipulative. Her charisma is misleading. She has expressed desires to kill others on numerous occasions and in her own best interests would be better off remaining in a secure hospital for the rest of her life.

Kira had escaped from the secure unit, taking her case notes with her. Like a chameleon she had changed her identity and blended in with society

Kira watched the notes go up in flames and then went back inside. Sally was ringing her on her mobile.

'Hi Kira, how are you doing? I've got some good news for you, the CPS have decided not to prosecute you. They have investigated the case and decided that you acted purely in self-defence. I am sorry for any stress caused to you and I wish you well in your future.'

'Thank you Sally,' said Kira politely, inwardly laughing at how easy it was to deceive people.

THE NEW PATIENT

Kira Devlin pulled into the car park of Portmead Hospital. She was looking forward to meeting her new patient, forty-year old Robert Dornan. She liked the beginning of new counselling relationships, so fresh and full of hope………

ABOUT THE AUTHOR

Berni Hellier was born and bred in Swansea, South Wales. She is married to Jon and has two amazing children, who will always be her greatest achievement in life. She has a fox red labrador called Woody who she adores. She first worked as a teacher and then as a counsellor.

She has always enjoyed writing. She wrote poems in her teenage years and began writing this novella when her children were teenagers.

Berni has also written some children's books, which will be published soon.

If you enjoyed this book please leave a review,
Many Thanks.

Printed in Great Britain
by Amazon

59272057R00111